Dove Song

Dove Song

Kristine L. Franklin

CANDLEWICK PRESS
CAMBRIDGE, MASSACHUSETTS

First paperback edition 2006

The Library of Congress has cataloged the hardcover edition as follows:

Franklin, Kristine L.
Dove song / Kristine L. Franklin. —1st ed.
p. cm.
Summary: When eleven-year-old Bobbie Lynn's father is reported missing
in action in Vietnam, she and her thirteen-year-old brother must learn
to cope with their own despair, as well as their mother's breakdown.
ISBN-13: 978-0-7636-0409-7 (hardcover)
ISBN-10: 0-7636-0409-7 (hardcover)
[1. Family problems—Fiction. 2. Mental illness—Fiction.
3. Brothers and sisters—Fiction.
4. Vietnamese Conflict, 1961–1975—Fiction.]
I. Title.
PZ7.F859226Do   1999
[Fic]—dc21   98-37621

ISBN-13: 978-0-7636-3219-9 (paperback)
ISBN-10: 0-7636-3219-8 (paperback)

2 4 6 8 10 9 7 5 3 1

Printed in the United States of America

This book was typeset in Goudy.

Candlewick Press
2067 Massachusetts Avenue
Cambridge, Massachusetts 02140

visit us at www.candlewick.com

Dedicated to the memory of my mother,

Virginia Harbord Brozovich,

who taught me to pray

K. L. F.

Chapter One

I *didn't expect* we'd move this time. Then one day out of the clear blue sky Mama sat me and Mason down and said, "We're moving up to Washington State tomorrow." I didn't ask why. I already knew. It was so we could be close to Daddy before he shipped out to Vietnam. His unit was scheduled to leave on September first, out of Fort Lewis. She told us on August twentieth. It didn't give us much time.

Daddy'd been transferred to the Sixth Army in June, so he could train a whole lot of new draftees. We didn't go with him because he said he wouldn't be gone that long, and besides, the Army planned to move him from base to base up and down the West Coast. He never said anything about going to Vietnam.

"Y'all stay put," he said. "I'll be back by the time school starts." He promised to write, and like every other time he went away, I felt my heart crack a little when he kissed the top of my head good-bye.

First he was in San Francisco. He sent us a postcard of Chinatown. Then they transferred him up to Fort Lewis. He sent us a postcard of Mount Rainier and one of a genuine Indian totem pole. Right after that he got his orders to go to Vietnam.

I remember the phone call because we were eating dinner, and me and Mason and Mama all had our mouths full of pork chop at the very instant the phone rang. Mama pointed at Mason, and he pointed at his mouth, and then he pointed at me, but my mouth was full too and the phone kept ringing and ringing, and I almost choked laughing because we looked like a bunch of fools. Mama answered the phone and swallowed hard. Mason let out a huge belch, but he was out of Mama's reach so all he got was an evil look.

"Hello?" said Mama. "Hi, Jimmy!" she said with the biggest grin you can imagine. "It's Daddy," she whispered to us. Her whole face lit up like it always does when Daddy calls. I knew how she felt. I finished chewing fast as I could. If I was lucky she'd let me talk to him for a whole minute. Long distance is real expensive.

Mama must have still had a little pork chop in her mouth because the next thing I knew she gasped real big and then she started choking and doubling over. I whacked her on the back. Mason jumped out of his chair and knocked it over. Mama stopped choking and stood up. First her face was red from choking, but almost instantly it turned white as paste. "When do you go?" she asked. "How long?" She listened and stared and blinked. "Okay," she finally whispered. "I'll tell the children." She hung up the phone without saying good-bye. I didn't get my minute.

"The president's ordered more troops to Vietnam," said Mama. She made her way to the table and sat down without looking at either of us. "Your daddy's going for a tour of duty. He'll be gone a year."

He'd said he would be training other army mechanics who were on their way to Vietnam. He'd said President Johnson was sending more and more troops but up till that minute I'd never once thought of my daddy as a troop. He wasn't a soldier. He was a mechanic, and a good one. He could fix anything with wheels and a motor. I'd seen the TV news about Vietnam, but that was far away and those were other men. Those were real soldiers, men who carried guns and grenades and tromped around in the mud. Daddy had an old shotgun that had belonged to his daddy, but personally, he didn't like guns much. Never did like hunting and such. One of his funniest stories was about being the worst shot in boot camp. The army makes a man into a soldier, but I'd never thought of Daddy as a fighting soldier. How could they send him to Vietnam?

Mason and I looked at each other and at Mama. She stared at her plate. Then she picked up her fork and started eating. What would Daddy do in Vietnam? Would he fix jeeps and trucks? Would he have to carry a gun? Would he write to us? Would we have to move again? Would Daddy have to fight? I didn't ask anything. It's best not to bother Mama when she's troubled. The rest of my dinner tasted like dirt. Two days after that she told us we were moving. She said she wanted to be as close as possible to Daddy, even if he was overseas, and besides, she was sick of Texas. It didn't cross my mind to ask questions.

At the time we were living at Fort Sam Houston, right

on base. We'd been lucky to get a house on base and Mama was happy because that meant we had a little extra spending money without her needing to work. Mama hates working. Once I heard her tell Daddy that ladies don't work, but he just got mad and said ladies didn't marry boys like him either and that was the end of that.

Before Fort Sam Houston, we'd lived in Georgia. That's where Mama and Daddy are both from. Before that, Oklahoma. Mama'd had to work there. Before that, Missouri. I was born in Texas. We've lived in Texas four times. Maybe that's why it felt more like home. Maybe that's why I didn't want to move. Or maybe it was because we would be moving without Daddy. We'd only get a few days with him, so we couldn't waste a single minute.

Mama and Mason and I packed boxes way into the night. I've packed so many times I could do it with my eyes shut tight. The boxes would be shipped after we left and had a new place to live. We packed our suitcases and one trunk, and the next morning we took a taxi to the Greyhound station. I didn't even get to say good-bye to my teacher, Miss McKenzie, or to a girl I'd started to swing with at recess. Her name was Julia. Her dad was a sergeant like mine. I wondered if she'd miss me. Probably not. We weren't exactly friends and besides, us army brats come and go. Everyone knows that.

It took three days and two nights to get to Tacoma, Washington. When we got there it was raining and my clothes smelled like diesel from all the bus stations we'd waited in along the way. Daddy always smells like diesel, from the trucks he works on. The diesel smell reminded me of him and why we were here and where he was going. For once I hated that smell.

Daddy didn't know we were coming. Mama'd wanted to surprise him. It took her two hours and half a roll of dimes to reach him. He showed up in a borrowed station wagon with a Fort Lewis sticker on the front bumper.

"I can't believe y'all are here," he said, hugging each one of us. He smelled like diesel, like always, like me from riding the Greyhound. I buried my face in his chest and fought the tears. When he hugged Mama I watched his face. He was worried about her. So was I. She doesn't do well when Daddy goes away.

Daddy'd gotten special leave for eight hours so we stayed at the Travelodge Motel that night. Daddy and Mama had the bedroom, and me and Mason had to share the pullout sofa bed. In the night I woke to the sound of Mama crying. I could hear Daddy talking to her, trying to calm her down. After a while the crying got worse and Daddy's voice turned harsh. "I told you not to move, Darlene. I told you there is no housing on base and nothing nearby. At least at Fort Sam you were practically next door to Jeri Lee. In case of dire need. She is family y'know." Mama's crying turned mad.

Why did Daddy have to mention Aunt Jeri Lee? He knew Mama wanted nothing to do with Aunt Jeri Lee, even if she was his only relative on the planet Earth and his baby sister to boot.

I've never met Aunt Jeri Lee. Mama would never allow it. It's a real touchy subject around our place, one of those things guaranteed to cause a fuss. One time I heard them fighting. Mama said Aunt Jeri Lee was nothing but a slut, and Daddy said all that is in the past and we got to forgive and forget and what do you expect from a girl raised in one foster home after another? Mama about went through the roof at that and here's why.

A while after Mama and Daddy were first married, when Mama was expecting Mason, Granny Brewer died real sudden and there was Aunt Jeri Lee, just fourteen, and Daddy wanted to take her in but Mama said no, not with a baby on the way. Everyone knew Jeri Lee was a wild girl, and Mama was not much older than her anyhow, so Daddy didn't push. There were some shirttail relatives, but they didn't want to take Jeri Lee, either. Nobody wanted her. She was just too bad.

Aunt Jeri Lee ran away from her first foster home when she was fifteen and got herself a baby but no husband—that's our cousin, Matthew Mark Brewer. He's between me and Mason age-wise. I've never seen him except in a picture. Daddy says a couple of years after Matthew Mark came along Aunt Jeri Lee tried to make good. She got a job waitressing and after a while she went to beauty school, but still, Mama didn't want us to have anything to do with her. Too low class.

After Aunt Jeri Lee got herself a real beauty parlor job, she sent us a Christmas card with two dollars, one for me, and one for Mason. There was a picture in that Christmas card too—Aunt Jeri Lee with ratted up light-blonde hair, and my cousin Matthew Mark in a red shirt. Mama didn't say a word when she saw that picture but she shot Daddy a look that said plenty.

I know there's more to the story. There always is with grownups. What's certain is that Aunt Jeri Lee is not welcome, and it's mostly Mama's fault, but Daddy goes along with it even though it makes him sad.

So why would Daddy bring up the subject of Aunt Jeri Lee now with Mama in such a state of upset? Why did he care so much whether we were close to family or not? Was it because of going to Vietnam? And what did he mean by "in case of dire need"?

Just then I heard Daddy tell Mama that she ought to make up with her own folks. Was Daddy crazy? Bringing up Aunt Jeri Lee was bad enough, but talking to Mama about her own folks—that was downright insane. I heard Mama holler, "Over my dead body," and then she sobbed so hard I could hear her gulping for air.

All I could do was stare at the ceiling and wish it would stop. After a while Mason turned over and poked me in the shoulder.

"You awake, Bobbie Lynn?"

"'Course," I said. Who could sleep through that?

"Sounds like Mama's starting up. Think it'll last long this time?"

"I don't know," I said. "I don't want to talk about it." Mason got up and went over to the television set. He flipped it on and we waited for it to warm up.

"You're going to get it," I said.

"I'll keep the sound down," said Mason. A test pattern appeared. Mason turned the dial. Another test pattern. "Think they have the Indian here?" he asked, and sure enough, the next channel had the Indian-head test pattern. "I wonder why there's never anything on TV in the middle of the night," said Mason. "I bet there's people who'd watch."

"Only stupid people would watch TV when they ought to be sleeping," I said. I threw a pillow at Mason but he caught it and threw it back. I grabbed his pillow and threw it at him. He caught it and threw it at me, but it hit the nightstand and knocked the motel alarm clock off with a bang.

"Hey!" yelled Daddy. "Y'all keep it down."

"Yes, sir," said Mason. He flipped off the television and climbed back into bed. Pretty soon his breathing became regular and I knew he was asleep. Mama was sniffing in the other room and I could hear Daddy's voice, just barely, saying, "It's all right, Darlene. You gotta be strong while I'm away. You gotta be strong for Mason and Bobbie. It's all right. Shh. It's all right." Mama'd never been strong, and she was always worse when Daddy was away. Daddy didn't know the half of it. Now he'd be gone for a year. Finally I fell asleep but I had a worried knot in my belly.

Daddy had to be back on base by six the next morning so he left before I woke up. We stayed at the motel one more night, this time without Daddy, and then the next day he helped us find a little house to rent. It came with furniture, but the furniture cost an extra fifteen dollars a month. I heard Daddy tell Mama that his paycheck would be bigger because of overseas and hazardous duty both so not to worry, but that only made her get pale and have to sit down. Daddy lit her cigarette. I don't think he knew how worried he looked or how worried I felt.

We had a few days in that house with Daddy home. He borrowed a car from his friend Bill and drove us around some. The night before he was due to ship out he came into my room and sat on the bed beside me.

"Hey, Baby Angel," he said, and messed up my hair. "I'm gonna send you some real good postcards this time." He petted my cheek over and over with one finger. His hands smelled like diesel. "You got your mama's pretty soft skin, you know that?" I nodded. I wanted to say a lot of things just then but my mouth was glued shut on account of holding in the feelings that went with those words. Daddy's hand was rough but I didn't care. His hands were always rough.

After a while Daddy slid off the bed and knelt on the floor beside me. His face was even with mine. "I gotta ask a big favor of you, Bobbie Lynn," he said. "Mama's gonna need a lot of TLC while I'm gone." Daddy's breath smelled like Crest.

"I know," I said. Mama always needed TLC when Daddy was gone.

"This time she'll need extra," said Daddy. "A year's a long time. You know how she depends on me."

"She depends on me and Mason whenever you're gone," I whispered. "We know how to get along fine." It was true. Daddy'd been away so much in the last few years that Mason and I had learned to do all kinds of things most kids don't do. When Mama was feeling down we did the laundry and the shopping and the cooking. Fact is, we did just about everything when Daddy was gone, but I didn't tell him that. I'd never tell him either. I didn't want him to think he couldn't count on me.

"Then I can be counting on you?"

"Yes, sir," I said. Daddy reached for me and I reached back. It was the biggest, longest hug I can ever remember but it was too short just the same. When he finally let me go he wiped his eyes on his sleeve.

"You write me a heap of letters, okay?"

"Okay," I said, and forced my face to smile.

He left for Vietnam the next day and school started and Mama went looking for a job.

Daddy always said moving around would give us advantages. He said we'd get to see a lot of good places most folks never see. He said we'd get our characters built up. And he said we'd learn to make friends real quick. That last part he only said because he makes friends real quick. Daddy laughs a lot and he's big and handsome and full of good naturedness. He's quick to make a joke, even if it's a joke about himself. Mason's like him in that. But not me. It's one thing Daddy never noticed about me. If I get one friend in a new place, it's pure luck. And Mama? She pretty much keeps to herself. Moving around isn't all that fun for everyone. And when you move because your daddy is going to Vietnam, well, it's worse than any other kind of moving.

School started a couple of days after Daddy shipped out and sure enough, not one single other girl in the entire sixth grade gave me any notice, except to be mean, that is. Northern girls are even worse than Texas girls mean-wise. That's why Wendy Feeney sort of surprised me. She ignored me but she wasn't mean. There's a big difference. Then one morning, around a month after school'd started, I noticed her staring at me. She smiled and then I smiled back, but we didn't speak. Not till the next day.

Chapter Two

I was standing over by the swings at recess, wishing I could get on and knowing that as long as I stood there waiting, the other girls would never get off, and I looked up and Wendy beckoned for me to come over. "Can you do this?" she asked, and then she tooted through her thumbs. I tried it a few times until I made the toot sound. "Yippee! I could tell you had good thumbs," said Wendy, and then she did a little twisty dance, right there in front of everyone. "Do it again," she said, and I tooted. "We sound like doves!" said Wendy. "Whistle with me, okay?" We stood in the middle of the playground and whistled. The whistling drowned out the sound of the other kids who teased.

"Yee haw! Ellie Mae!" they yelled. They knew my name was Bobbie Lynn, but they called me Ellie Mae because of my double name and because of *The Beverly Hillbillies* show. They said I talked with a hillbilly accent. To me, *they* all had accents.

I'd moved a lot, but I'd never lived in the North. I was the new kid in Mrs. Saunder's sixth-grade class, the new kid with a hillbilly accent and the ugliest hair in all of Washington State.

The day before school started Mama'd cut my hair into a pixie. She said she wanted me to be in style with the other girls at my new school. She'd read it in a magazine and tried to copy the picture. 'Course I wanted to fit in, so when I saw myself in the mirror with hardly any hair left I bit my lip and decided it was worth it. Turns out Mama was dead wrong. Not one girl had a pixie like me. Most of them wore their hair long, with a headband to keep it out of their face. No one looked like me. I was the tallest girl in the class and like Mama says, I'm on the generous side. The teasing started right away. Except, like I said, for Wendy.

Wendy Feeney was in my class. She sat up two rows and over one, right in the front. Kids called her Teeny Weeny Wendy Feeney, because she was as short as a third-grader and as skinny as a matchstick. Sometimes they just called her Weeny. I could tell she hated it. Whenever anyone said it, her face turned red and she made her hands into fists. She avoided other kids at recess, kind of played by herself, like me. Maybe that's why she finally came over. We were outcasts so we had something in common. I'd never expected her to teach me to whistle like a dove.

"You whistle good," she said when we took a break from tooting. She had a little voice to go with her little self, high and squeaky like a cartoon fairy. I said "thanks" though I felt shy, and then Wendy said, "I like the way you talk, Bobbie Lynn Brewer. You sound just like President Lyndon B. Johnson."

"He's from Texas too." Right then it felt good to be from Texas.

"You have to hold your thumbs like this to get a better sound," said Wendy. "Try it." I bent my thumbs a little like she'd suggested. "Good thing you have short hair," she said when a long, curly, black strand of hair blew in her face and got stuck between her thumbs. I smiled and then I whistled again and again until I was nearly out of breath. We whistled together for the rest of lunch recess, except for once when we took a break to rest our lips and wipe the spit off our thumbs.

On the way back to class Wendy said that when she whistled by her back fence at the same time each afternoon, a whole flock of white doves would appear out of nowhere. A girl named Debbie heard her say it.

"You are such a little liar, Weeny," said Debbie. "There aren't any doves around here."

"There are too," said Wendy. Her voice sounded even higher and I saw her hands turn into fists.

"Filthy old pigeons aren't doves."

"They aren't filthy," said Wendy. "And pigeons and doves are the same kind of bird, you stupid. The birds that fly over my house are white. White DOVES."

"Liar, liar, pants on fire," said Debbie. She smiled in a mean way.

"I am not a liar!" shouted Wendy. "Doves, doves, *doves!* Want to fight about it?" Her sharp little jaw jutted toward Debbie and I could hear her breath coming fast, in and out of her nose. "I'll slap your ugly face."

"You're a lunatic," said Debbie. "Like the rest of your crazy family. You should watch out, Ellie Mae. The Weeny is a loony bird."

"Doves, doves, *doves!*" Wendy said it again, this time

like a chant. She circled around Debbie. By this time a whole pack of kids was watching. I felt frozen to the ground. "Doves, doves, *doves*," said Wendy, right in Debbie's face, until Debbie blushed and shrugged and walked away. Wendy stuck her tongue out at the rest of the kids and turned her back. My heart was fluttering in my chest. Maybe they were right. Maybe Wendy *was* a loony bird. She grabbed my elbow.

"There really are doves," she whispered. "They fly over my house at four-thirty every day but only if I call them. Do you believe me?" I looked down into Wendy's face. Her eyes were wild and my elbow hurt where she was hanging on for dear life. I nodded and Wendy relaxed her grip. "Are you very good at skipping?" she asked, and then she took off skipping across the blacktop. I stood in one place and watched. Girls our age hardly ever skip anymore, especially when other kids are watching. Wendy skipped in a huge circle all the way around me. Then she skipped up and said, "Skipping is sort of like flying because you're in the air part of the time." She was out of breath and her chest heaved in and out. "You're good at dove whistling," she said. "Did you know that angel wings sound exactly like a whole bunch of doves?" I shook my head.

"I know a lot about angels," said Wendy. "I'm practically an expert. I learned from Father Rossini, in my other school. Everyone has an angel. Even you. Haven't you ever heard your guardian angel at night? Haven't you heard its wings? Don't you ever feel it pat your cheek or mess up your hair in the wind?" I didn't know how to answer such strange questions. All I knew was that Daddy always called me his baby angel, and thinking about doves that sounded like angels made me think about him. Maybe there'd be a letter waiting when I got home.

Right then the bell rang. Recess was over. Debbie spoke to one of her friends as she passed me and Wendy. "Looks like the Weeny finally has a friend as weird as herself. Did you see them hooting through their hands?" The other girl giggled and tossed her head.

"Weeny must have learned it in *Pittsburgh*," said the other girl. Wendy grabbed my arm again. Her face was blotchy with anger.

"Pittsburgh is way, way, way better than Tacoma-Stinky-Aroma, Washington State," she said through clenched teeth.

"Is that where you're from?" I asked.

"Yeah," said Wendy. "And we're moving back any day now. All my friends are there. If I could fly like an angel, I'd be there in ten seconds." Suddenly Wendy spread her arms like wings and started to run toward the other girls. "I'm a dive bomber! Watch out!" she yelled. As she passed the girls she grabbed a handful of Debbie's blonde hair and yanked.

"I'm telling!" yelled Debbie, rubbing her head. Wendy didn't look back. She flew like a bird all the way into the school building. I thought about Debbie calling Wendy a loony bird. Maybe there was something to it.

I didn't get a chance to talk to Wendy for the rest of that day. When I got home I got the notion to whistle through my hands one more time, right before I went into the house. I hooted four or five times but not a single bird showed up.

Chapter Three

That night when I went to bed, right before I made a tiny pencil mark on my bedpost, I imagined an angel like a huge, beautiful bird, hovering over me and beating its wings to fan away the stuffy air in my room. I said a prayer, like Mama taught me when I was little. Just before I fell asleep, I thought I heard the soft sound of feathers brushing against my quilt. I told Mama at breakfast.

"You got the craziest imagination, Sweetie Pie," she said without looking at me. She blew two smoke rings toward the ceiling. "As far as I know, angels just fly around in heaven." Poor Mama, I thought. Her eyes were bloodshot and she smelled like old hair spray. It looked like she hadn't slept a wink. Mama tended to get that way, especially when she was having one of her delicate spells. When she was feeling good she was pretty as can be. She had shiny dark hair and light blue eyes and dimples on both sides of her mouth. She always said it was a shame Mason got the dimples instead of me. She looked so bad just then. Daddy leaving was enough to make anyone upset. No wonder.

I told her about Wendy and how the other kids thought she was strange, and how she'd almost started a fight on the playground.

Mama said I ought to stay away from such an ill-mannered child. What she meant was stay away from that trashy girl, but it wouldn't have been polite to say so, and Mama's particular about manners.

"I think she's all right, Mama," I said. "She's new too, like me. She's from Pittsburgh. She says they're moving back real soon."

Mama blew smoke and took a drink of her coffee. I was just about to tell her how none of the other girls had a pixie haircut when my big brother Mason started griping because there wasn't any lunchmeat left. Mama frowned hard at me. "Did you eat that lunchmeat, Bobbie Lynn? I told you not to get into it."

"Yes, ma'am, it was me who ate it," I said, staring into my bowl of oatmeal. I felt my face turn red. I'd eaten the last piece after school the day before. I knew I wasn't supposed to, but sometimes my stomach is just one big, empty hole. Mama sighed and told Mason he'd better take tuna fish, and Mason slammed the refrigerator door and swore. Mama said she was going to get the belt so Mason slipped out the back door. He winked at me on the way out. We both knew Mama wouldn't beat him. She never did. I bit the inside of my cheek to keep from laughing.

Mason was getting awful bold with his sassing these days, but only because Daddy wasn't around. Mama didn't do a thing. Poor Mama. I'd tell Mason to let up later. Mama needed our help. Just looking at her it was easy to see she was feeling poorly.

After Mason left, Mama wasn't in the mood for talking about haircuts or angels or anything. She mashed out her cigarette and said she was going back to bed. She'd found a job and was working swing shift and didn't get home until midnight. No wonder she looked tired. I made two tuna sandwiches and left one on the counter for Mason, in case he came back. Then I left for school.

At morning recess not one single girl talked to me except Wendy. She skipped up with a big sunny smile on her face and said we should practice whistling. I still hadn't decided if I should play with her or not. She didn't look trashy to me, even if her hair was a mess. "Come on, Bobbie Lynn," she said. "You're a great whistler."

"The other girls said it sounded like hooting."

"The other girls are stupid jackass idiot weirdo big-butts." Wendy said it with a straight face, but there was a bad little twinkle in her blue eyes and I couldn't help but bust out laughing. I agreed to whistle, for a while anyway. We whistled for five minutes but then right in the middle of whistling Wendy stopped and whispered, "Idiot weirdo big-butts," and that gave me a giggle fit so bad I couldn't whistle another note.

"When did you move here?" I asked.

"Last January," said Wendy. "Right after Christmas. My dad lost his job at the steel mill. Now he works at the smelter, but only until they're hiring again in Pittsburgh, which will probably be any day. I can't wait to leave."

"We move all the time," I said. "I'm used to it." I was used to my friends moving at the drop of a hat too. So why did it give me just a twinge of sadness that Wendy would be moving soon? I hardly knew her. We weren't really even friends, not yet. I should be used to it. I guess the truth was, I expected we'd move all the time, and I expected the people I liked would move too, but it was still a surprise when it happened.

"This is my first time moving," said Wendy. "And I hate it, except I'm glad my dad has a job at the smelter for now."

I knew where the smelter was. Daddy had pointed out the big brick smokestack to us one afternoon when we went for a drive in Bill's car.

"Lotta folks think that's where the bad smell comes from," he'd said.

"That's why they call it the SMELL-ter," said Mason.

"Don't interrupt, Mason," said Mama.

"The smell comes from the paper mills down on the waterfront," said Daddy. "Not the smelter."

"What's a smelter?" I'd asked.

"It's where they make metal from ore," said Daddy.

"No, it's what I say when Bobbie Lynn lets one," said Mason. He made a rude sound. "Peee-yew! Guess I smelt her." He slugged me in the arm and doubled over laughing until Mama reached around behind and smacked him on the top of the head. It didn't hurt him a bit. I could tell by the look on his face. He had to cover his mouth to keep from laughing.

"No son of mine is gonna talk like that," muttered Mama.

"Leave him be, Darlene," said Daddy, smiling and patting Mama's arm. Mama jerked her arm away. The car swerved and Mama cried out. Daddy straightened the wheel. I looked out the side window at the houses going by.

"He deserved it," said Mama. "He sounds like white trash."

"Just like me?" said Daddy.

"I never said that," said Mama.

"Yeah, well your daddy thinks so. Maybe you do too."

"Don't talk about it, Jimmy." Mama turned and looked out her window. "Just let it be," she said quietly.

For a minute it was like we were all frozen there in the car like statues. Bringing up Mama's family was a recipe for trouble. Daddy'd ruined the whole drive. Didn't he know better by now?

Once when I was five Daddy explained it to me and Mason. See, Mama's from a ritzy family in Georgia. Her own daddy was an army colonel which is pretty high. Everyone called him The Colonel. Mama got sent to fancy schools and all. She was even a beauty queen at one of them—the Rutherford Girls' Academy Peach Queen. She still has the crown.

When Mama was seventeen she met this West Point boy when he was home on leave, and she was supposed to marry him and there was an engagement party and all, but later on he went to Korea where there was a war and he got wounded. Daddy said he got his legs blown clean off. I don't know if Mama wouldn't marry a legless boy or if the legless boy wouldn't marry her or if her parents wouldn't let her marry him. Anyhow, they didn't get married and right away Mama turned around and met Daddy and fell head over heels in love, and it was not fine with her folks that he was a GI and a mechanic and that his own daddy had died serving time.

Mama and Daddy eloped and then the fat hit the fire and Mama got disinherited. The old Colonel told Mama she was as good as dead to them for marrying bad. That was the end of Mama ever talking to her folks again. That's what Daddy told us. And that was why me and Mason'd never met our granddaddy and grandmamma Perkins. Colonel Perkins. I'd never seen him, not even in a picture, but I knew I wouldn't like him if I did.

Daddy reached over and turned up the car radio. It was playing a Beatles song.

"Anybody want to go to the zoo?" asked Daddy. "I heard they have an aquarium and seals and even a couple penguins." Mason and I said we did, but Mama didn't say anything so Daddy drove home and no one said a word until we got there.

"I'm going to the laundromat," said Mama. Daddy tossed the keys across the car seat to her. I got out before I saw her take them. She drove away except she didn't take any clothes with her. Daddy left two days later for Vietnam.

I told Wendy about moving from Texas. She asked if I'd ever seen a rattlesnake and I said sure, but only a dead one. By the time recess was over, she'd asked about tumbleweeds, oil wells, cowboys, and the Alamo. On the way into the building Wendy asked me to come over after school. "You could see the doves," she said. "No lie."

"I never said you were lying," I said.

"I know," said Wendy, "but I bet you wondered." It's true, I'd wondered, but for some reason I dearly wanted to see those doves, maybe just to prove snooty Debbie wrong.

"I don't know if my mother'll let me," I said.

"Just ask her like this," said Wendy. "PLEASE PLEASE PLEASE PLEASE PLEEEEEEEEEEASE? and for sure she'll say yes."

"I don't know. She just started a new job and I can't call her unless it's an emergency."

"Then she won't even know if you do come over," said Wendy. "Right?" I nodded. Mama wouldn't be home until midnight, maybe later.

"Maybe," I said. "Only maybe."

Wendy immediately told everyone I was coming over. Debbie and the rest had plenty to say about that.

"If you think the Weeny is bad, you should see her retard sister," said Debbie, and then she and her friends crossed their eyes and stuck out their tongues like snakes. "They must've dropped her on her head."

"Can't even talk."

"She's a *vegetable*."

"Weeny pushes her around in a wheelchair, all over the neighborhood."

"They should keep the retard at home."

"Ellie Mae will fit in good at that house," said Debbie. "Retarded girls all have short hair, so they don't eat it."

"*Shut up!*" shouted Wendy, and the other girls laughed. Wendy was shaking mad. "You are the most horrid,

disgusting girls in the universe to make fun of my sister!"
Wendy had tears in her eyes. I wished I had the nerve to
yell at those girls like she did. I wanted to tell them to
shut up too, but I didn't want them to call me worse
names so I kept quiet and thought about what they'd said.

I saw a retarded boy once, when I was seven. We were
at a parade. He wore a football helmet and sat in a
wheelchair and when anyone walked past him he yelled
"Stop that!" Mama whispered in my ear not to pay any
attention to him. She said not to stare so I tried not to
look but my eyes were like magnets to that boy in the
helmet. She said he was a poor little retarded boy and
couldn't help how he acted. "Stop that!" he yelled when
a clown walked past giving out candies. "Stop that!" he
yelled when the Shriners drove by in their funny hats
and little cars. "Stop that!" he yelled when another boy
next to us started to whine because he couldn't ride the
fire engine.

"Stop that," mimicked my brother Mason in a
quiet voice. He giggled. Mama and Daddy gave each
other looks.

"Those folks should leave that boy home," said Daddy
out of the side of his mouth.

"Isn't that the truth," said Mama. "They should be
ashamed to take him out in public like that." I remember
being glad I wasn't retarded because if I were, Mama'd
leave me home. Then I remembered thinking maybe the
boy shouting "Stop that!" was having a good time and
maybe his parents were glad he could see the parade even
if he did seem strange to others. Just then the boy

drooled on his shirt and didn't wipe it away and I felt embarrassed all over for him. Maybe Mama was right.

"We'll have a ton of fun if you come over," said Wendy. We were out by our lockers in the hallway after school. She tooted softly through her thumbs. "The doves will love hearing both of us."

"I don't know," I said. "If my mom finds out I went somewhere without asking I might get in a heap of trouble."

"Would you get grounded for a month or something?"

"Yeah, something," I said. I wasn't sure what. There was no telling what Mama might do these days, now that Daddy was gone. Most likely she'd start to cry. Sometimes when that happened I wished she'd actually get   out the belt. A licking would be better than watching her cry any day.

"All right," said Wendy. "Maybe not today, then." Her eyes were as pitiful as a hound puppy's. We said good-bye and I started for my house. I thought about that boy who yelled "Stop that!" Did Wendy's retarded sister yell? Did she eat her own hair? I wasn't sure I wanted to find out.

Chapter Four

When I got home the doors were locked. I tried the windows but Mama had shut them up tight the night before on account of rain. Mason was supposed to come straight home after school to let me in. Then he was supposed to get right to work on his homework. I was plenty big enough for a house key of my own, but Mama said I was too young. Now here I was, stuck waiting for my ugly brother.

I sat on the steps for a while hoping Mason would hurry up, but he never came. He already had a couple of buddies. I figured he was with them. He'd probably forgotten all about letting me in.

When the paperboy dropped off the *News Tribune* I knew it must be nearly four o'clock. That's when I decided to go see where Wendy lived. Why should I have to sit on the front porch until kingdom come? I started off down the block.

First I walked past Wendy's house instead of going in. What if her mom didn't want me to visit? Mama didn't usually like us to bring friends over. She said extra kids means extra racket. Me and Mason had learned a long, long time ago to keep quiet when Mama was feeling delicate. I hoped Wendy's mom wouldn't mind me too much.

What if Wendy's retarded sister was around? The thought made me feel jumpy. Would she yell "Stop that!"? I went around the block once. Twice. Did Wendy really want me to visit? Maybe she was teasing. All the other girls were mean to me. Maybe she was mean too and I was too stupid to know it.

A train blew its whistle somewhere far off just as I was about to pass Wendy's house the third time. The sound made me think about the doves and that skinny, mop-haired, freckle-faced Wendy who'd said I had an angel. I ran up the steps and rang the doorbell.

"Hey," said Wendy with a smile as wide as a water-melon, "You came!" She grabbed my hand before I could say hello and pulled me inside. "You have to meet every-one," she said. "That's Stevie," said Wendy, pointing to a boy building a house of playing cards on the coffee table. "Don't talk to him while he's concentrating. And that," she said, pointing to a red-haired baby girl crawling across the floor with a plastic dog in her mouth, "is Therese." Wendy took the dog out of Therese's mouth. "No putting dirty things in your mouth," she scolded. "Bad girl." The baby crawled over to where Stevie was working and reached to pull herself up.

"Don't touch!" screamed Stevie. He didn't once take his eyes off the cards. Therese turned and headed in another direction.

"He's concentrating," explained Wendy. Stevie looked like a fourth-grader, or maybe third. He had four layers of cards and was working on the fifth. Wendy dragged me across the room.

"Lookit, Jean," Wendy whispered. "Look who's here!"

There on the sofa lay a girl. It was hard to guess how old. Maybe eight or nine. She was thin, like she hardly ever ate a thing, and her hair was cut short and curled around her face like black lace. Her empty eyes stared at nothing. They rolled back and forth, pausing for a moment on each side. I swallowed. I could hear my heart beating in my ears. I'd never seen a retarded person up close before.

"This is Jean," said Wendy. "She's blind but she can hear real good." Wendy reached down and picked up one of Jean's hands. She held it against her own cheek. "Who's this, Jean? Who's me?"

Jean moaned.

I felt my heart skip a beat.

"Is she sick?" I whispered.

"No," said Wendy with a big grin. "She's mad because I didn't introduce you properly."

"Miss Bobbie Lynn Brewer, meet Miss Jean Feeney," said Wendy. "We're twins," said Wendy. "Can't you tell?" I looked at Wendy and then at Jean. Was she joking? How could they be twins? One was bouncy and liked to whistle through her thumbs. The other was . . . what had the mean girls said? A vegetable.

"Twins? Really?" I squeaked.

"Yep. Her name is really Mary Jean, but my mom's name is Mary too so we call her Jean."

"Jean is . . . um . . . a lot smaller than you," I said. Now I could see some resemblance in the face.

"She was born first," said Wendy, "but she's always been smaller. Even I'm pretty small for twelve, if you haven't noticed. We had our birthday last week. See the cards on the mantel?" I glanced over at the fireplace. There was a neat row of birthday cards. "Stevie arranged them."

"My birthday is next month," I said. "November twentieth." I was itching to ask if Jean had always been retarded but I knew it would be impolite. Had someone dropped her on her head like the mean girls said? I guess Wendy read my mind.

"Jean wasn't born this way," said Wendy. She patted Jean's hand and played with her fingers. "When we were three months old we had our vaccinations and something went wrong with Jean's. She almost died. Now she's like this, but at least not in heaven. Not yet, huh, Jean?" Jean jerked her hand away and moaned loudly. "Oh, sorry," said Wendy. "Rude old me. I didn't finish." She turned toward Jean. "Bobbie Lynn has yellow hair, the same color as dandelions, and she's way taller than me and she's from Texas. She's still only eleven."

Wendy took a checkered handkerchief from the arm of the sofa and wiped a shiny bubble of drool from Jean's pink mouth. "Jean gets mad when we don't tell her what new people look like."

Jean rolled her blue, blue eyes in my direction. How could she know what dandelion-colored hair looked like? I watched her face. Her eyes moved back and forth, back and forth. Maybe she *was* blind, but I felt like she could see me just the same, that she could see I felt pretty funny to be staring down at a little retarded blind girl with spit on her lips. If I'd stepped on ten pieces of chewed-up Juicy Fruit I wouldn't have been more stuck to that wood floor than I was right then.

"You can talk to her," said Stevie. He was still staring at his card house. Wendy watched me.

"Hi, Jean," I whispered. "Nice day."

"Wah," said Jean.

I blinked.

Wendy clapped. It made Jean startle. She turned her face in Wendy's direction. "She likes you!" Wendy grabbed one end of the sofa. "Gimme a hand," she said. "Stevie, get over here and help. Jean loves to see the doves."

"I can't help now," said Stevie.

"This *second*," said Wendy, and Stevie dragged himself away from the coffee table.

"My dad put wheels on the sofa so we could push Jean around," said Wendy. "She's getting too big to carry places." Wendy pulled. I pushed. It wasn't nearly as heavy as I'd thought. Stevie pushed too. We wheeled Jean through the kitchen and out through some glass doors and down a little ramp to the backyard. We parked Jean on the patio and Wendy's brother went back inside. A plump woman with petunia-pink cheeks and short hair as black as a crow's belly flapped a blanket out the door at us. "Wendy!"

"That's my mom," said Wendy. "Mom, this is my new friend, Bobbie Lynn."

"Hi, Bobbie Lynn," said Wendy's mom.

"Pleased to meet you, ma'am," I said.

"Girls, if you're going to take Jean outside you have cover her up."

"It's not cold, Mom," said Wendy, but we took the blanket and covered Jean anyway. Wendy tucked her in all around. Just then I heard a loud yell inside the house followed by hysterical crying.

"That stupid card house," said Wendy, shaking her head. "I bet Therese got it. It happens every day. It's a wonder he doesn't give up."

"Why doesn't he do it someplace else?"

"I don't know," said Wendy. "He's got his way of doing things and there's no talking him out of it." She rubbed her hands together. "He'll stop screaming soon enough. Let's see if we can get the doves to come. Get out your whistler!"

I cupped my hands the way Wendy'd shown me, thumbs together and bent just so. I licked my lips and blew until the sound came out clear, the sound of a dove, like the song of an angel, at least that's what Wendy said.

Ooooo-EE-ooooo-EE-ooooo.

Wendy blew through her thumbs.

Ooooo-EE-ooooo-EE-ooooo.

We crossed the yard slowly, whistling, singing the dove song, until we came to the fence. Behind Wendy's yard was an empty field. Wendy pointed up with her chin and I knew this must be the place the doves would come from.

Ooooo-EE-ooooo-EE-ooooo.

We whistled until I felt dizzy and spit dribbled between my thumbs. I stopped for a second but Wendy shook her head so hard I only had time to wipe my hands and start up again.

Ooooo-EE-ooooo-EE-ooooo.

I looked sideways at Wendy but she didn't see me. She was staring at the sky like there was nothing else in this whole wide world that mattered more than getting the doves to come.

Ooooo-EE-ooooo-EE-ooooo.

We whistled *Ooooo-EE-ooooo-EE-ooooo.* We were a dove duet without the doves.

I was right in the middle of an *Ooooo-EE-ooooo-EE-ooooo* when Jean started to laugh. I stopped whistling until Wendy grinned and nodded.

Don't stop now, she was telling me. *Not now. Keep on whistling.*

So we whistled.

Ooooo-EE-ooooo-EE-ooooo.

Jean laughed, and laughed, and laughed.

It was the kind of laughing that makes your cheeks twitch; the kind that makes your mouth want to grin and your belly want to hoot.

Ooooo-EE-ooooo-EE-flurpf.

It was hard to concentrate with Jean laughing like that.

I stopped to take a big, deep breath. Wendy kept whistling. I wiped my thumbs on my dress.

"Look, look, *look!*" whispered Wendy. She had stopped whistling and was pointing across the field.

A long way off, beyond the field, beyond the houses, a flock of white birds rose to the sky from behind a tree-covered hill. I counted as fast as I could, but I couldn't keep up with them and after thirty-two I lost count. Higher and higher they flew, one huge cloud of fluttering wings. They moved in a kind of dance, flying together first to the left, then to the right, circling higher and higher, moving in our direction as they did.

"Now watch!" said Wendy. "Watch what they do!"

Two birds broke away from the flock and flew even higher than the rest. Three more followed them up. When it seemed they could go no higher, they suddenly fell toward the ground as though they'd been shot and were fluttering down to die.

"What happened?" I asked. I felt like I'd been hit in the stomach. "Is somebody hunting them?" How could anyone kill those beautiful white birds?

"Watch, watch!" said Wendy. The birds fluttered down, turning and tumbling out of control and then suddenly, as if they'd come instantly back to life, they flew back up and joined the rest of the flock.

"Why do they do that?" I wondered out loud.

"I don't know," said Wendy, "but they do it every day." More birds flew up and fluttered down. The flock flew overhead. "Hold your breath and listen," Wendy whispered in my ear. I held my breath and stared above our heads. The flock of doves flew in a wide circle and I could hear the beating of their soft, perfect wings.

"Bub!" yelled Jean from her couch. The sound made me jump.

"Listen, Jean," said Wendy. "Just listen to them." Jean was quiet for a few seconds, until the birds were out of earshot. Then she spoke quietly.

"Bub," she said.

"That's right," said Wendy in a soft, soothing voice. "That's right!"

We watched as the flock flew over the garage and circled far to the east, until they were just white dots against the blue autumn sky.

"What'd you think, Bobbie Lynn?" cried Wendy. "I *told* you the doves would come!"

"You were right," I said.

"Yeah, and can you believe the giggle-puss?" said Wendy. She pointed her thumb in Jean's direction. I looked at Wendy's sister Jean on her sofa. Wendy leaned up close and whispered in my ear. "Sometimes she laughs so hard I have to stop whistling because I'm about ready to wet my pants."

I looked at Wendy. Her nose was only two inches away from mine. There were probably a hundred and one freckles on that pointed nose. I'd never seen freckles so close. I looked over at Jean. Her face was freckled too. I hadn't noticed before.

"Why does she say 'bub'?" I asked.

"It's her word for birds," said Wendy. "Up until a month ago, she only said a few things that sound like words. She says 'ma' and 'dah' and I think she means 'Mom' and 'Dad' but Mom and Dad say it's just blabber. I don't care what they say. I try to teach her words anyway. And Miss Newcomer reads to her—Miss Newcomer is Jean's baby sitter once a week when my mom and the other ladies from the Sacred Heart Circle go to clean a convent where a bunch of real old nuns live. Miss Newcomer taught kindergarten for a hundred years and she says any child can learn, even a slow one. She just loves Jean, and Jean's about as slow as they come. Anyway, most of the time nothing happens and then look! Now Jean says 'birds.' I told Mom it's a miracle. I can't wait for everyone in Pittsburgh to hear."

"When are you moving back?" I asked.

"Oh, in a month or two."

I looked at Jean again. Her eyes were closed and she was smiling.

"What does Jean call you?" Wendy frowned and turned away to look out over the empty field.

"Nothing," said Wendy. "She doesn't have a name for me." She stopped talking for a few seconds and then she whirled around. "But she said 'birds.' Isn't that wonderful? You heard her didn't you? You're a witness."

"I sure did hear it," I said. I watched Wendy cross the yard to sit beside Jean on the couch. Now Jean looked like she was asleep. Maybe 'bub' meant birds. Maybe not. I'd have to be two eggs short of a dozen to argue with Wendy Feeney and think I'd get anywhere. I watched as she pulled the blanket up around Jean's face and patted her gently on the shoulder.

"Come over again, Bobbie Lynn," said Wendy. "Promise you'll come back tomorrow."

The first few weeks of school had been lonely. I looked at Wendy's eager face and knew I had a friend at least for a month or two, a friend who could whistle up a flock of doves out of no place. Could be she was a speck on the nutty side, but even a crazy friend was better than nothing.

"I'll promise to try," I said, and I truly meant it.

Chapter Five

Jean didn't wake up even when we pushed the couch back up the ramp into the house. We put her in the living room and then I followed Wendy into the kitchen. Wendy's mom gave us graham crackers and green Kool-Aid with paper straws. I watched while she mixed up a bowl of meat loaf big enough to feed the entire Sixth Army. She let Stevie break an egg into the bowl. His eyes were still red from crying. The baby, Therese, held on to his leg and watched while he did it. Wendy's mom mixed and mixed, squishing the meat and raw eggs and bread crumbs between her fingers. Wendy drank her Kool-Aid until she made slurping noises with her straw.

"Jean said 'birds' again, Mom," said Wendy.

"I'm not sure she really means anything by it," said Wendy's mom. "It could be just a noise."

"I think it's just a noise," said Stevie. "Wendy says it's a miracle."

"Oh, I don't know about a miracle," said Wendy's mom. "It's a miracle that Jean is still with us. That's enough of a miracle for me." Wendy rolled her eyes.

"Sister Mary Immaculata said miracles still happen all the time," said Wendy.

"Well, I wouldn't want to disagree with Sister," said Mrs. Feeney, "but there's such a thing as facing reality too, you know, Katie."

"Katie is me," said Wendy, answering my question before I'd had time to ask it. "It's my middle name and it's all Mom's fault." Wendy shot a grin at her mother. "Mom wanted to name me Wendy, after the girl in *Peter Pan*, but Dad said it isn't a saint's name and he wanted Kathleen, so they made a deal and Mom got to pick the first name but Dad got the name they called me. Get it?" I nodded. "So everyone called me Katie up until we moved here and I told everyone to call me Wendy instead. It's my new identity."

"You look the same as before," said Stevie. "You should get a disguise if you want a new identity. Like wax lips."

"I had to pay him a quarter to start calling me Wendy."

"You still *act* like Katie," said Stevie.

"If you call me Katie I'm taking back my money." Stevie stirred his Kool-Aid. "Everyone in Pittsburgh calls me Katie. Except Sister Mary Immaculata. She always called me Wendy Kathleen, the whole thing. Sister Mary Immaculata was my fifth-grade teacher. She's eighty years old."

"Oh, surely not eighty," said Mrs. Feeney.

"Yeah, Mom, because she told us she was born in 1888, in Ireland. This is 1967 so that means she was eighty last year."

"Wrong," said Stevie. "She was seventy-eight."

"I was *rounding*, Mr. Smarty Pants," said Wendy.

"You can't even subtract," said Stevie. He stuck out his tongue.

"You stink, Stephen."

"Enough," said Mrs. Feeney. "Mind the temper and the tongue, Kate."

"School was free there, if you were in the parish," said Wendy. She looked through the straw at me and a green drip splashed on the table. "Here it's twelve whole dollars a month. Can you believe it's that expensive? That's why I have to go to public, where all the girls are creeps, except you, I mean. When we move back I'll be in Sister Mary Saint Pierre's class."

"We're not moving back," said Stevie. "Dad said." I looked over at Wendy. She pressed her lips together tight and gave Stevie the dirtiest look on Earth. Stevie stuck his tongue out.

Wendy turned to her mom. "I still think it's a miracle. Jean talking, that is."

"Mmmn," said Mrs. Feeney. She shaped the meat into a loaf and put it into a big glass casserole dish.

"Exactly fifteen hours and fifteen minutes until school tomorrow," announced Stevie.

"Stop that!" said Wendy. "Or I'll bop you on the bean."

"Mom," whined Stevie, "she's threatening."

"Girls, would you please peel potatoes?" Wendy's mom handed us a sack of potatoes. She acted like she hadn't heard Stevie. We took the potatoes to the sink and Wendy started washing.

"Where do you go to church?" asked Wendy. "We go to Holy Rosary. We're Catholics." She wiped her hands on her clothes and pulled a necklace out from under her blouse. It was a little gold cross with Jesus on it. "This is how you can tell a Catholic," said Wendy. "Our crucifixes have Jesus on them. Other people just have plain crosses." She tucked the crucifix away and went back to washing potatoes. "What are you?"

I felt my face turn red. "We don't go anywhere." That's what I told Wendy. What I didn't tell her was that we used to be Baptists, up until I was in third grade.

When we were little Mama took us every Sunday, no matter where we lived. She made us say our prayers at night and read us stories from a picture Bible, and when I turned eight she got me my own white Bible with a zipper around the edge. The zipper had a cross on the end, one without a Jesus.

Daddy never did go to church. It was one of the things Mama and him fought about. Mama thought all decent folks should go to church. Daddy said he could be a decent fellow without having to put on a suit and tie every Sunday. "The Good Lord don't care if I'm sitting in a pew or not," he said. Mama said the Good Lord did care, but Daddy just laughed. So she took us herself. I liked Sunday school and I liked that white Bible a lot.

When I was in third grade Daddy went away on his first real long job. Mama fretted something awful, and made us say extra prayers. After a while she was too tired to do just about anything, including go to church. We were in a new place and we didn't know hardly anyone. We'd only been to that church a couple of times.

At first, when we didn't come to church anymore, some of the ladies came by to check on us, and the minister too, Brother Ray, but after a while no one came over. They were all strangers and Mama didn't want them around. She smoked and worried and took a lot of naps. She cried too, almost every night, though she tried to hide it from us back then. I knew. I could tell by her eyes the next morning.

In a while Daddy came back and we moved again, and we never did go back to church anywhere, though Mama always kept her Bible by the bed. I'd only been to church one time since then and I didn't want to tell Wendy about it. It was that awful night me and Mason were away from home.

"Where do y'all keep the potato peeler?" I asked. Wendy pointed to a drawer and I dug around in the knives and utensils until I found what I was looking for. I grabbed the red wooden handle of the peeler and set to work on a big potato.

Daddy was somewhere in Missouri doing what he always does, training mechanics. Seems like he was gone a long time. Mama was really bad off. She'd cry and stay up all night. Then she started going for walks. She'd leave the house and say, "I'm going for a walk," and she wouldn't take her purse or anything and we never knew when she'd be back. Usually it was late.

Anyhow, one night she didn't come home at all, and we were so scared. The next morning Mason said we should go to school, just like normal, and not to tell anyone, but I didn't listen. I told my teacher, Miss Elaine. Miss Elaine asked could our grandparents or an aunt or uncle come get us after school and I said no. I didn't tell her about Aunt Jeri Lee. And Mama's folks? Well, that was a sore spot. I knew not to tell Miss Elaine all our family business.

Next thing I knew a policewoman came and got us out of school. Boy, oh boy, was Mason mad at me. They took us to a foster home and all I could think of was my aunt Jeri Lee and what happened to her and how bad she turned out.

We were only there for overnight but it felt like a year to me. The foster-home people were the Johnsons and they took us to church even though it wasn't Sunday. There was lots of singing and a man in a suit waved a Bible in the air and yelled. I couldn't tell if he was mad or not. It wasn't like Baptist Sunday school. I didn't like it. I suppose the Johnsons were nice people, but I didn't like them, either.

The next day a social worker came and took us back home. Daddy came home a few days after that, but before he did Mama made us swear not to tell him. She said she'd been out walking and got lost and confused but now she was fine and not to tell Daddy or he'd be upset with her. She said she was sorry and cried a lot and we swore not to tell. It was one of her real bad delicate times, the worst one I could remember. We were used to keeping her spells private from outside folks, but it was the only time we'd kept it private from Daddy. I didn't like it, but I did it because I'd sworn.

"I *asked* what your dad does for work," said Wendy. "Were you day-dreaming or something?"

"Sorry," I said. I felt my face turn red.

"He's in the army," I said. "He's a mechanic. He's in Vietnam right now." It felt strange talking about Daddy.

Mama hardly spoke of him being away. We'd had one postcard so far. I hoped a big pile of real letters would show up soon. The postcard was from Hawaii. It showed three girls in hula-hula skirts. Mama tossed it on the table and went upstairs to her room right after she read it. I took and put it under my pillow. The hula-hula girls were pretty. Daddy said he missed us and that Honolulu was as muggy as a swamp in August. He said it was good practice for Vietnam.

When Daddy shipped out to Vietnam Mama didn't even go to the base to say good-bye and that's a first. "He'll be back before we know it," she'd said. She was fine for the first week but after that the trouble started. First it was smoking way more than usual. Then it was pacing at night, and crying. I could hear her through my wall. When she wasn't fidgeting or fretting or yelling at Mason she was sleeping or staring out the window. Her worry was eating her up, and it made me worry too.

Mama hadn't bought groceries for days. It's like she forgot we needed to eat, and didn't want to eat herself, so Mason and I started fixing this and that for ourselves. I'd hoped maybe now that she worked at a grocery store that'd change. Each night I made a pencil mark on my bedpost, counting the days until Daddy would come home, counting the days until Mama would be happy and fine again. Every night I said a prayer that Daddy would be safe. But I hadn't talked about him being gone. Not a word.

"When did he leave?" asked Stevie. He was sitting at the table, stacking graham crackers.

"Around a month ago," I said.

"Exactly a month? To the day?" asked Stevie.

"Hush, Stephen," said Mrs. Feeney.

"I hope your dad shoots a lot of communists," said Stevie. "I hope he blows their heads off and stabs 'em in the guts with his bayonet. *Ka-POW!*"

"STEPHEN!" shouted Mrs. Feeney. I jumped and my arm knocked two unpeeled potatoes off onto the floor. "Shame on you, *shame*." For a second there wasn't a single sound in that kitchen, until Therese plopped herself in the middle of the floor and started to cry. Wendy picked up the potatoes and started peeling. I wished I were small enough to crawl into the saltshaker. Stevie was going to get it. I waited for the sound of a slap but it didn't come.

"My dad was in a war," Wendy whispered in my ear. "In Korea. He never talks about it, though."

"I don't want any talk of killing in this house," said Mrs. Feeney. "Understand?"

"But if the Americans don't kill the communists, Russia and China will take over the world," said Stevie. His voice was pouty. "I don't want to be a communist. That's why I said it."

I'd heard Daddy say the communists wanted to take over the world. It's why he'd signed up again, even when Mama cried and begged him to get out of the army once and for all. I remember that night well enough.

"I got a duty, Darlene," said Daddy. "That's all there is to it." I'd been so proud of him then. He was patriotic and brave. Communism had to be stopped no matter what. But that was before they sent him to Vietnam.

"Communists or not," said Mrs. Feeney, "I don't

want to hear you talk about killing people like that again. War is a terrible thing. A terrible waste. Terrible." She shuddered and took a deep breath. "Say you're sorry, Stephen."

"Sorry."

"And I'm sorry I yelled at you. I'm sorry, Bobbie Lynn," said Mrs. Feeney. "Sorry to lose my temper like that and I am sorry your father is overseas. You must be worried for him. I'll say a prayer tonight."

"Thank you, ma'am," I said, letting my breath out all at once. I didn't realize I'd been holding it for so long. At my house, if Mama yelled about something it usually ended with her staring out the window and crying for a couple of hours. She never apologized. And she never got over it right away.

Little Therese was still blubbering but no one paid any attention to her and pretty soon she crawled off to the other room. We finished the potatoes and Stevie asked, "How many did you peel?"

"Would you *quit?*" asked Wendy. "Let's get out of here." We left the kitchen and went into the living room. Wendy crossed to where Jean was still sleeping on the couch. She pushed Jean's thin legs over and made room for herself. "Quit hogging the whole couch, Jean. Sit, Bobbie Lynn." Wendy patted a space beside herself. "Sit over here." It felt strange to sit so close to someone who was sleeping, but I did as Wendy said, sitting carefully so as not to touch Jean. Wendy leaned right up against her.

"Don't feel bad about my mom yelling," said Wendy. "Certain people can be a real pain." She pointed at Stevie, who had just sat down in front of the coffee table.

He didn't seem to hear Wendy's comment. He picked up a playing card and looked at it.

"That's all right," I said. "My mom yells too." Truth was, nowadays she downright screamed if any little thing went wrong, like Mason dropping a fork at the table or me forgetting to wipe my feet, but I didn't want to tell Wendy that part. I listened to Jean's breathing. It rattled a bit. How could she sleep with two people sitting next to her and talking? I watched Wendy rub Jean's back. She smiled as she touched her sister and snuggled closer in to her.

The last time I'd snuggled close to anyone was when Daddy knelt beside my bed that night before he left. It wasn't a month exactly. It was thirty-two days. Right then it seemed like forever.

There were some people who said America had no business fighting in Vietnam. Daddy called them yellow-bellied liberals. Once there was a show on TV about some college students who were protesting sending soldiers to Vietnam. They wouldn't go to classes and they wouldn't go home. They just sat down and wouldn't move. Some of them burned an American flag and Daddy got so mad he threw Mama's ashtray right at the TV. Good thing the ashtray was plastic. The TV didn't break but there were ashes all over the rug. Right before Daddy switched off the TV, I heard one college student yell that President Johnson should be kicked out of the White House for sending men to die overseas. Now Daddy was there because President Johnson had sent him. Would he get hurt? Would he—

"Do you think your dad will get killed?" asked Wendy,

interrupting my thoughts. I swallowed but didn't say anything. "You do, don't you? I can tell by looking at you, Bobbie Lynn. I'd be scared too." Wendy's breath smelled like green Kool-Aid. I could only stare. "You should ask his guardian angel to take extra special care of him if you're scared. Ask. Ask right this very minute."

"I don't know," I said, feeling all of a sudden trapped on that sofa with Wendy, not wanting to talk about Daddy or angels or being scared.

"Remember how I said everyone has a guardian angel?" Wendy's bright eyes searched my face. I felt my cheeks turn hot. I remembered what the kids at school had said about her being crazy. "Don't you believe me, Bobbie Lynn?" she asked. "You don't, do you? It's true."

"Oh, golly, look at the time," I said, looking over at the clock above the fireplace. I stood up to leave. "I have to go home now, all right?" I turned and took a step. The vibration shook the coffee table enough to knock over several playing cards.

"Why did you do that?" yelled Stevie.

"I'm sorry," I said, wanting like anything to get out of there.

"Just shut up, Stephen," said Wendy. "Shut *up!*" She leapt to her feet and pulled on my shoulder to turn me around.

"Why don't you believe me?" asked Wendy. "About your dad's guardian angel. He has one. He does." A lock of curly black hair fell forward into her face. "It's the truth!"

"Well, it's just that angels and all, maybe that's for Catholics," I said. "I'm not sure we have guardian angels, and besides, I have to go now, cross my heart." Wendy grabbed both my hands.

"Father Rossini said everyone has an angel, every single person, not just Catholics. Father Rossini knows *everything*. He's so cool. All the kids love him. He played football at Notre Dame." She squeezed so hard my fingers hurt.

I felt a lump form in my throat and I tried to swallow it down. Everything had been so happy and fun before, when we were whistling in the yard and drinking Kool-Aid. Now I couldn't wait to get out of that house, away from Wendy and her sister on the couch and her strange little brother with his cards. I wanted to get away from Wendy's wild eyes, away from her mother who could go from nice to yelling to nice, just like that. I didn't want to hear about angels or talk about going to church and I didn't want to think about my dad fighting in a war because communists were going to take over the world. A whole hornet's nest of feelings had been stirred up in my heart and I had to get away.

I pulled my hands away. "I'll see ya," I said. Then I turned and let myself out the door and down the steps.

"You promised you'd come back and whistle for doves," called Wendy. "And Jean did say 'birds.' You heard it. She only did it because you were here. She was showing off, you know. She really liked you." Her voice was farther away now. "You promised, Bobbie Lynn. You promised."

I ran all the way home. I ran so hard I could barely catch a breath. The breeze had picked up and as I ran I heard Wendy's voice in the wind. "You promised, you promised, you promised." By the time I got to my house, I was cold all the way to my bones, and the feelings in my heart were as jumbled together as the junk under my brother Mason's bed.

Chapter Six

When I found Mason washing dishes I knew something was wrong. I'd come in the back door all out of breath, into the kitchen, and there he was, up to his elbows in suds. It was my week to wash.

"You're supposed to dry and put away this week," I said. Mason didn't turn around.

"Where've you been?" he said. His voice sounded funny, higher than usual.

"At a girl's house," I said. I noticed a cigarette smoldering in Mama's kitchen ashtray. It was almost down to the filter. "You got to quit sneaking cigarettes, Mason," I said. "Daddy says you can't smoke until you're twenty-one." But as soon as the words were out I knew it couldn't be him. There was lipstick on the filter end. My heart sank. Mama was supposed to be at work.

"Mama's home early from work," said Mason. I felt guilty all over for going to Wendy's.

"Is she sick?"

"Not exactly," he said. He didn't turn around. "How come you didn't come home after school?" He was scrubbing the oatmeal pan from breakfast. I stared at his back. His voice. It was so strange, like the words were being choked off before he could get them out. I wondered if he'd gotten in trouble himself.

"I did come home. You weren't here to let me in." Mason could be so bossy. All because of being thirteen and thinking he was big. I was just about to tell him to mind his own beeswax when the house was filled with a wailing sound, like a cat with its foot caught under a tire. My heart jumped into my throat. I saw Mason stiffen up.

"Mama's upset," he said. "She's having a bad spell. Just keep your mouth shut." I held my breath and froze as the sound continued. What could be wrong? Was it her new job? Mama never did last long at a job. She said working every day was too hard on her nerves.

"No, no, no, NO!" cried Mama, and then more wailing. I looked at Mason. He turned around. His face was dead white.

"What—," I started to speak but Mason cut me off.

"Quiet," he said. He was panting, like a dog out of breath. He looked eight years old again, not thirteen. "It's real bad this time. I never saw her this way. It's worse than ever before. Way, way worse." The wailing got louder and higher. I stepped close to my brother. Now I could feel my heart pumping clear up in my head. My stomach made itself into a hard ball. I wanted to run away from that awful sound, but my feet wouldn't move.

"Noooooo," came Mama's voice, this time closer. Then she screamed just like a witch and said a string of terrible curse words. Mama never swore. Never. I jumped a foot into the air and Mason grabbed me and pulled me close. I could feel his heart racing.

Mama burst into the kitchen. Her eyes were red and there were black streaks where the mascara had run down her face. She was still in her bright orange Piggly Wiggly uniform.

And she was carrying Daddy's shotgun in her arms.

"Hey now, Mama," said Mason, like he was talking to a baby. He shoved me behind him. I hung on to his shirt and buried my face in his back. He shook so hard it rattled my head. "Put down that old gun, Mama, please?" he whispered.

"I knew how to load it," said Mama. Her voice sounded odd—low and raspy, and way older than thirty-two. "My daddy taught me how. My daddy was a colonel in the U.S. Army, you know."

"Gimme the gun," said Mason. His voice squeaked. "Please?" Now I could hear a smile in his voice.

"No," snapped Mama. She staggered a little. I felt Mason shake his head, then I felt him back into me, back a little, backing me up, slowly, one small backward step and then another. I clung to him. I smelled his sweat. I heard a click and then I opened my eyes and peeked around in time to see Mama point the shotgun at the ceiling. "God deserves it," she said. "For what he's done to me."

God? My slow brain could make no sense of her words. I saw Mama's finger squeeze the trigger. It felt like watching a slow-motion movie.

"Mama!" shouted Mason.

BOOM! My heart felt like it burst inside my chest. Mason shoved me to the floor. I bit my tongue and tasted blood.

Dying. I'm dying. Right now.

BOOM! Pieces of ceiling plaster and dust rained down on my back. My eyes were squeezed shut so tightly that they felt like burning holes in my head.

We're going to die.

I don't want to die.

I don't want my brother to die.

Mason had dropped to the floor and he was halfway lying on me. I could feel him breathing hard.

Breathing.

I was breathing too.

Not dead yet.

Mama whimpered. "He's never done me any good," she said. "He deserved it."

Did she mean God? Isn't that what she'd said? How could anyone kill God?

Mama began to cry. I heard the gun fall with a clatter to the linoleum floor and looked up. The kitchen was filled with gunpowder smoke and dust. There were two huge holes in the ceiling. I tried to get to my hands and knees but it was hard because I was shaking. Mason scrambled forward and grabbed Daddy's shotgun. He slid it across the floor. It bumped into my hand.

"Shh, Mama," said Mason. "It'll be all right." I could tell he was trying real hard not to cry himself. He put his arm around Mama and helped her up. "Go on and lie down," he said. "Then you'll feel better. Me and Bobbie Lynn'll clean up the kitchen. Nobody's hurt."

"Then I missed him?" said Mama like a child, like a sad, bitty girl. "I never could shoot straight."

"Now just forget about guns and shooting," said Mason. "You need to sleep."

"I can't sleep," said Mama. "I can't." Mama shuffled out of the kitchen like a zombie, sobbing and hiccupping and saying she was sorry for shooting God.

I felt like I was watching a horror movie. My heart was still pounding. My head hurt. I tried to stand up but my knees collapsed under me and I sat down hard on the gritty floor. "What's going on?" I squeaked. I made the panic stay out of my voice. "What happened to Mama?" Tears filled my eyes. Mason ignored my question and slumped into a chair. He put his head down on the table. "What is going *on*, Mason?" I yelled. I couldn't stop. I heard my voice like it was coming from some other girl's mouth. "HOW COME MAMA WANTS TO SHOOT GOD?" Mason was crying hard. His whole body shook. I stood up and crossed to him on wobbly legs. I pounded him on the back. "TALK TO ME, MASON BREWER!"

"Daddy," he blubbered. "It's Daddy."

I grabbed his shoulders and felt my fingers dig deep into the muscle. "TELL ME RIGHT NOW!" I screamed in my big brother's ear. He lifted his head and turned halfway around. Tears had made streaks in the dirt and dust on his cheeks.

"They went and called Mama at work," he said.

"They who?" I begged. "Make sense, you idiot boy!" I slugged him as hard as I could on the shoulder. He didn't even seem to feel it.

"They're supposed to tell you in person," he said.

"They're supposed to send an officer to your house. I saw it in a movie." He was blubbering now.

"What are you talking about?" I dug my fingers into Mason's shoulder and shook him.

"Daddy's MIA," he whispered. "Missing in action."

Mason's words shook me harder than any shotgun blast ever could. MIA? Daddy? "No, Mason," I said. "It's a lie."

"It's no lie," he said.

I closed my eyes and clung to Mason. In my mind I saw Mama with a gun pointed at the kitchen ceiling, pointed toward God, and suddenly my stomach flip-flopped like a dying catfish on the riverbank. My knees gave out again and I sank all the way to the floor.

Mason cried quietly for a while. I stared at his shoes. His feet were so big. I thought about Mason's big feet until it reminded me of Daddy saying by the time Mason was all the way grown we'd have to call him Bigfoot.

Where was Daddy now?

The tears ran down my face and dripped off my chin.

What would we do about Mama?

After a while Mason nudged me with his knee and said, "We'd best clean up this mess."

Chapter Seven

I got a cleaning rag and ran the water in the sink as hard as it would go, wishing the sound would drown out the pounding in my brain. I stared into the sink and watched the water go down. I don't know how long I stood there like that, but suddenly Mason was shoving me out of the way and splashing water on his face. He grabbed a dishtowel and rubbed the dust off his head. "Someone's at the front door," he said. He snatched a dishtowel out of the drawer and dried his face. He grabbed my arm and pulled me close. "Don't you say one word, you hear me?" I nodded. He pushed the towel into my hands and hurried out to the living room. The doorbell rang twice. Someone knocked.

"Oh, hi there, Mr. Steward." Mason's voice was as phony and cheerful as could be. I crossed to the kitchen doorway and listened. I could hear our neighbor talking, but I couldn't hear what he was saying. All I could hear was my brother.

"Yeah, that was us, sir," he said, and then he laughed. "Me and Bobbie Lynn were trying to cook some of that real hard squash, you know, the hubbard kind—Mama told us to have it for dinner and usually we do it up in the oven, and well, sir, we put it in the pressure cooker thinking that would be quicker and we must've done something wrong because the whole blessed thing blew up. Sounded just like a bomb, didn't it?"

A pause. "No, sir, Mama doesn't want us to use the pressure cooker so I hope you won't tell her . . . no, sir, no one was hurt. We were in the other room watching TV. I'd be ashamed for you to see the mess we made . . . squash all over the ceiling." He laughed again. I thought I heard Mr. Steward laugh too. "We'll get it cleaned up before she comes home from work," said Mason. Another long pause. "Thank you, sir," said Mason. "We won't ever try it again, don't worry." The door closed. I peeked around the corner in time to see him take a deep breath and slump against the wall. He buried his face in his hands.

"You big fat liar," I said. He looked up and his face was as pale as a ghost's. I'd heard Mason fib plenty of times, but I'd never figured on him being such a champion liar.

"If anyone finds out what Mama did they'll come take us away."

"What are you talking about?"

"You know." *Like when they took us to the Johnsons. Like they did to Jeri Lee when Granny died.* I didn't say it and neither did he.

"We have to protect Mama, take care of her. She needs us more than ever. You don't want them to lock her away, do you? Other people might not understand about her moods."

"What are we gonna do?" I whispered.

"Clean up the mess," said Mason. "And take care of Mama until she's feeling better . . . ," he swallowed hard, "and until they find Daddy." He crossed the room to me and put his hands on my shoulders. "We aren't going to tell a single soul. That's what we're gonna do. You got that?" I looked up into his scared eyes. "Swear."

"I swear," I said.

"You'd better not tell, like you did last time," said Mason. "Mama's just upset on account of Daddy being . . ." He bit his lower lip and looked away. I swallowed down the sob that was creeping up my throat just then. Mason took a breath and continued. "You know how delicate she is and I guess it just shocked her to get the news and anyhow, they'll find him, then we'll tell her and she'll be fine. She's just having a bad day." He let go of my shoulders and turned to go into the kitchen. "Help clean up."

A bad day? Going after God with a shotgun and shooting holes in the ceiling was way more than a bad day. I felt new tears creep up into my eyes. "Mason," I said, "what if they don't find Daddy?" He froze in his tracks but didn't turn around.

"Don't you ever say that again," he said. "Hear me, Bobbie Lynn? Not as long as you live." His voice cracked. "Now go get the broom."

It took us more than an hour to clean up. First thing Mason did was take the shotgun down to the basement. I didn't ask what he did with it because I didn't want to know. I picked up the big pieces of plaster and put them in a Piggly Wiggly bag. Then I swept and mopped. Mason stood on the kitchen table and washed off the ceiling around the big holes. He picked off the pieces of plaster that were hanging and tossed them down to me. I wiped the countertops and the table, the seats of the chairs. I climbed up on the sink shelf and took down the kitchen curtains. I took them out and shook out the dust, but the gun smell was still in them. I wadded them up and left them on the back porch. All this time neither of us said a single word. It was like we were robots from an outer-space movie. The loud buzzing in my ears made me feel like a machine. It also kept me from thinking about anything but cleaning up Mama's mess. Oh, I remembered about Daddy being missing, but I didn't let myself think about it up close.

We couldn't fix the holes in the ceiling. Mama had missed the light fixture, so there weren't any wires or anything, just holes with splintered wood and plaster. Mason cut up another Piggly Wiggly bag and taped the paper over the holes with masking tape. Even though the holes weren't hurting anything, I was glad he did it. Just looking at them made me feel sick and scared.

I was propping open the window over the sink when I heard Mama's voice. "Bobbie? Mason?" I turned around and there she was, standing in the kitchen doorway looking white as a bed sheet. Mama had put her hair in a French roll for work. It was still pinned up, but there was a lot of hair hanging around her face. Mama was always so careful about her hair. She had a strange smile on her face.

"Hi, Mama," I said. Mason was out in back, putting the bag of plaster pieces in the trash can. "Are you feeling better?"

Just then Mason came in the back door. Mama looked at him and kept smiling. I saw two tears splash at her feet. The three of us stood there and did nothing, said nothing. I felt those two covered-up holes staring down at us. Mama sniffed and wiped her eyes. "I heard someone at the door," she said finally. "Was it Daddy?" Her voice was tiny, like the voice of a pitiful child.

I heard myself gasp. Mason elbowed me hard.

"No, Mama, it wasn't him," said Mason with a smile. "It was just the paperboy, right, Bobbie?" I nodded but no one saw me. I'd never heard my brother so cheerful and helpful. Usually he was a sassy smart-mouth, and lazy as could be. And I'd never heard my mama so mixed-up.

I'd never heard my own heart beat either, not until now. Everything was upside down and unreal, like a bad, bad dream.

"Take her upstairs, Bobbie Lynn," said Mason. I forced my legs to move me across the kitchen.

"Come on," I said. I put my hand on Mama's arm. She was shaking hard, sobbing and wiping her eyes. "It'll be all right, Mama," I said. I took her hand and led her upstairs. I helped her lie down and covered her with her pink bathrobe. She turned and sobbed into the pillow and I reached out to pat her back, but before I could touch her she rolled over and stared at me with the saddest eyes I've ever seen.

"Where's Jimmy?" she asked. Her question felt like a

whack in the head. How come she didn't remember? What was I supposed to say?

"He's, um, stationed overseas," I said. "He's fine. He is." I made my voice cheerful like Mason's. Was that the right way to lie? Wouldn't Mama know I was lying? I never was a good liar and Mama knew it. She didn't notice this time. Another sob tried to choke me but I forced it away.

"He could be dead over there," she said. "They say missing but they mean dead and they don't tell you." Now she remembered. Mason had been right. She was just shocked by it all and no wonder. I wanted so bad to make her feel better.

"Maybe they've already found him, Mama."

"They LIE!" shouted Mama. I jumped up and away from her bed. My heart fluttered in my chest like a bird's heart. I felt my breath catch in my throat. I backed out of the room and shut the door. Then I leaned against the wall and slid all the way down to the floor.

I sat there for a long time and listened to Mama. She sobbed and whimpered and talked to herself. I put my hands over my ears and pressed hard, so hard it hurt, but I could still hear her. I tried to drown out Mama's sobs and the sound of the other voice in my head. It came from a dark place in my mind, a black bottomless pit where all the ugly monsters in bad dreams live during the day.

Dead. Dead, dead, dead. He couldn't be dead. *Go away!* I told the terrible thought. I pushed harder on my ears until my whole head ached.

"Cigarettes!" I jumped at Mama's voice. "Get me my

cigarettes." I ran downstairs and rummaged through Mama's purse on its hook by the door until I found her cigarette case. I ran back up and went into her room. Now she was sitting up in bed.

Mama sniffed and reached for her cigarettes, pulled one out, and lit it. Her lips wrapped around the filter end and she drew in a deep, smoky breath. "You know," she said with a strange smile, "a lot of movie stars smoke." I grabbed an ashtray off the dresser and handed it to her. "I could have been a movie star, if I'd wanted to."

"I know, Mama," I said. My heart was still pounding from running up the stairs. My hands shook. My mouth was as dry as a bone. Mama giggled. I caught my breath.

"Smoking makes a woman look so glamorous. That's why I started."

Mama inhaled deeply and started to cough. She looked terrible, not even a little glamorous. Daddy'd always tried to get her to quit. He never let her smoke in bed. I was too scared to remind her. I didn't want her to ask me any more questions about Daddy.

Right then I had to get out of that room. "Just holler if you want anything, all right?" I said. Mama blew smoke at the ceiling and tapped her cigarette on the ashtray in her hand. Tears rolled down her face and dripped off her chin. When I closed her door she was still smiling.

When I got into my bed I didn't make a mark on my bedpost. I didn't say that prayer from when I was little because right then God was nowhere to be found. And I didn't hear any angel wings either.

Chapter Eight

The next day Mason told me I had to stay home with Mama. "Just to make sure she doesn't do anything." We were in the kitchen and I could still smell the gunpowder and plaster dust.

"You should stay home," I said, trying not to sound as scared as I felt. "You're older." I didn't want to be alone with her. What if she asked me about Daddy? What if I had to tell lies? Poor Mama. She was so sick, and I knew she needed me, but how could I stay there all day? Mason wouldn't give in.

"Do as I say, Bobbie Lynn. I have a test in health class today, a first-aid test, and the teacher said if we miss we flunk. We have to act normal or people will ask questions. Don't let anyone in the house and don't tell a soul what she did." His eyes rolled up toward the ceiling and then he looked at me. He must have seen that I was scared. "I hid the gun," said Mason. "Just take care of her now. You know I'll help when I come home, like always."

"But what about me missing school?" I asked. "That isn't normal either." We'd never had to stay home from school to care for Mama before and it gave me the willies. "I don't want to get in hot water. Playing hooky's against the law."

"We'll trade off," said Mason. "But get one thing straight." He came over and stuck a finger in my face. "Now that Mama's not doing so good, I am in charge, hear?"

"You aren't my boss."

"I am now. Mama needs us ten times more than she did those other times." Mason was right. All the other times we'd just done a lot of extra work—shopping, cooking, housework, even going to the laundromat—but always Mama was there, asking us to do this and that, saying she was too tired, reminding us to keep the noise down. I didn't want Mason to boss me, but I didn't want to be the boss either. "You're just gonna have to do what I say," said Mason.

"You're such a pig sometimes," I said. I didn't want Mason in charge of me, even if he was older, and I didn't want to miss school, but mostly I was scared to be with Mama without Mason there. I didn't want to tell him that. He'd just act big. He left for school without making a sandwich. As the door closed behind him, I wondered what he'd eat for lunch.

It was strange being home from school. I watched game shows mostly. I wondered if my teacher would know I was playing hooky. Would the school call? What would I tell them if they did?

Mama slept most of the day. I peeked in on her whenever I heard a sound. She was still in her uniform. Once she was sitting up smoking and I said, "Mama, want to put on your nightie?" and she said yes but didn't move.

I had to help her undress, like she was a baby, and it made me so embarrassed I could've died. I'd never seen Mama without her clothes, not ever, and she didn't care one bit that I was there. When I unhooked her bra in the back my hands were shaking. She looked so pale and thin, so pitiful. She'd always been delicate, but this was so much more than that. How long would this terrible spell last?

There was one thing good about staying home. Worrying about Mama kept me from worrying about Daddy.

The phone rang twice that afternoon while I was watching soap operas. Both times I about jumped out of my skin. I thought for sure it must be the principal of my school, Mr. Janesziek, calling to say I was in big trouble but it wasn't him. The first call was a lady from the base asking if she and some of the other ladies could bring over dinner for a few nights. She'd heard about Daddy too but she wasn't anyone we knew. I said no, that Mama wanted to be left alone and the lady said she understood completely. She said to call if Mama needed anything and she gave me her phone number.

Then Mama's boss at Piggly Wiggly called. I took a message for Mama. I told him she was sick in bed and he said he hoped she'd be well soon. She was sick, and she was in bed, so it wasn't a lie.

I watched the hours creep past in slow motion. At three, I started looking for Mason. At three-thirty he still wasn't home. At three-forty-five, the doorbell rang.

Just then I heard the back door open and slam hurried to the kitchen. "Someone's at the door."

"Who is it?" asked Mason. He had just opened book bag and was taking out some cans of food. I s. Spam, Campbell's soup, canned spaghetti, and two cans of evaporated milk.

The doorbell rang again. "Should we answer it?" I asked, worried that someone else besides Mr. Steward might have heard the gunshots. Mason went out to the living room.

"It's a man in a uniform," said Mason.

"Police?" I squeaked.

"No, army." The doorbell rang again. "It's probably news about Daddy!" I walked into the living room just as Mason was letting the man into the house. "We just got home from school," he said. "I hope you weren't out there long, sir."

Would it be bad news? Worse than Daddy being MIA?

"My name is Captain Bruce Hedges," said the man. "Is your mother home?"

"She is, sir," said Mason. "But she's all laid up from the bad news about my father." That part was true. I listened and wondered what lies Mason would have to tell.

"I need to speak with her," said the captain.

"She asked to be left alone, sir," said Mason. "And she was pretty firm about it, but she said I was to take any messages. I'll make sure she gets all the information you have for her." He stood up very straight. I could see his face was white.

Don't let it be worse news.

"I'm Mason Brewer and this here's my sister, Bobbie Lynn." Captain Hedges looked at me and then back at Mason, then he nodded slowly. I held my breath.

"All right then," he said. "I'll trust you to tell her what we've found out about your dad." I bit the inside of my lip. Don't let it be bad. I felt so dizzy I had to sit down. My ears were ringing but I made myself listen to their conversation. I didn't say a word myself.

Turns out Daddy was on a supply flight and the plane he was in got shot down. That's all they knew. The man said there was a lot of jungle around there and that there was a good chance Daddy was alive because as far as they could tell, the plane didn't burn, but of course he could be hurt, or he could be captured and of course they were doing everything they could to find him and the other men. When he said that part I let out my breath with such a *whoosh* that both Mason and Captain Hedges looked at me. I felt my face turn red.

I'd heard the words, and I knew he was talking about Daddy, but it felt like I was listening to the radio or the TV. Jungles, helicopters, antiaircraft guns—that was TV stuff. But at least he wasn't dead, not for certain. Suddenly, without any warning, I heard myself asking a question.

"How long will it be before they find him?"

"I don't know that," said Captain Hedges. "A few days, a week, maybe more. I'm sorry I don't know the answer to that." He looked at his hands and fussed with his cuffs.

"Thank you, Captain," said Mason. He let the captain

out and I heard them both say good-bye. "I'll go up and tell Mama," Mason said when he came back inside. He ran up the stairs. I followed behind him and stood in the doorway while he told her everything Captain Hedges had said.

At first it looked like it wasn't sinking in, but suddenly Mama started to shake all over. Then she was crying hard but then all of a sudden, like she'd switched gears into reverse, she started to laugh. At first it was just a little giggle. Then she started to laugh right out loud, like she'd just heard the funniest joke in the world. The sound of it made my blood run cold. I looked at Mason and he looked at me. I never saw his eyes so big before that. We hurried out and shut the door. I swallowed down my fear. Mason was breathing so hard he looked out of breath. Mama's laugher turned into crying and we went downstairs to the kitchen without saying a word.

I cooked soup and fried-up sliced Spam. I didn't ask where Mason got the food but I was positive he'd stolen it. He didn't have any money of his own and he'd be too proud to ask any of his friends for a loan. I didn't accuse him of anything. He would only get mad at me, and besides, I didn't want to hear him say it. Somehow I knew that if I didn't hear the words, it wouldn't feel so bad that my brother was a thief. I knew why he did it. No one could know we were out of food. No one could know about the holes in our kitchen ceiling. No one could know how Mama was acting.

Mason gulped down the food. I couldn't eat a bite. Even though I felt nervous about going up there, I took some soup up to Mama's room. She was lying on the bed with her eyes open, but it didn't seem she'd seen me come in. "Mama?" She blinked and turned away. The smell of the food made me feel sick. "Mama, you have to eat something." How long had Captain Hedges said? A few days, a week, maybe more. How long would we have to coax Mama to eat?

"I need a cigarette," she mumbled.

"No," I said, surprised at myself for talking back. "You have to eat first." I expected her to scold me but she didn't. I took the half-empty pack of cigarettes from her nightstand. "If you eat all that soup I'll give you back your cigarettes, okay?" Mama turned her back on me. I fought the tears that sprang unexpectedly to my eyes. "I mean it," I said, like I was talking to a three-year-old, not my grown-up mother. I left the room as the first tear slid down my cheek. Girls aren't supposed to talk to their mothers like that, like they were the mother and not the other way around.

Why did treating Mama like a child make me feel so little? I closed the door and went to my own room. I put Mama's cigarettes on my dresser. They didn't look right there.

I wiped my tears with a corner of my bedspread and fanned off my face. When more tears wanted to come because I could hear Mama crying again, I dug my finger-nails into the palm of my hands until it hurt too much to remember the nightmare happening in our house.

Inside my head, just behind my eyes, those tears wanted to come. I had a terrible feeling that if I let them out maybe I'd never stop crying, so I bit my lip again, hard. And then I bit the skin on my thumb until all I could think of was that terrible strong pinch. The pressure behind my eyes let up some, but still, my eyes felt like they were burning. I rolled off my bed. There was work to be done.

After I cleaned up the dishes Mason and I watched *The Flintstones* and then I went to check on Mama. The soup bowl was empty and she was sleeping. I got the cigarettes out of my room and put them back on her nightstand and pulled her covers up so she'd stay warm.

On the way downstairs I noticed Mama's purse hanging on its hook. I slipped it off the hook and took it to Mason. I handed it to him and without saying a word he took out her billfold and removed all the money from it.

"How much do we have?" I asked. Mason counted.

"Twelve dollars and seventy cents."

"If you get caught stealing food they'll arrest you," I said. Mason's green eyes met mine. Mama always said Mason had cat eyes. *And then everyone will know about Mama.* I didn't say that part. I didn't need to. He looked down, like he was ashamed. Then I saw him set his jaw and stare right at me and I knew I'd hit the nail on the head. He would steal if he needed to, just like a stray dog. He'd do what he had to do to survive. Well, so would I.

I went back to the kitchen and ate a bowl of crushed soda crackers with evaporated milk poured over them. While Mason watched *The Man from U.N.C.L.E.*, I called Mama's boss at the Piggly Wiggly.

"This is Darlene Brewer's daughter," I said. "My mom won't be coming to work for a few days, maybe a whole week, because she has a very bad kind of flu with a lot of throwing up." I felt my face burn from the lies but I had no choice. Mama's boss wanted to know who was taking care of us. "My aunt Jeri Lee," I lied. "She's coming tomorrow." My voice caught in my throat and for a split second I wished it were true.

Mama's boss told me Mama hadn't worked there long enough to get any sick pay, so the days she missed would be without pay. I said I understood. When I hung up the phone my mouth was as dry as the desert and my hands were shaking. I finished watching the show with Mason but I don't remember what it was about.

Just before nine Mama's bedroom door opened and we heard her walk down the hall to the bathroom. The toilet flushed, the water in the sink ran, the door opened, and she went back to her room. That's the first night she started rocking. We heard something scrape across the floor in her room. Then we heard the *thumpity thumpity thumpity* of her old rocking chair going back and forth.

Mama rarely used the chair. It was the only thing she had from her own family. She always said it was ugly but she'd hauled it around every time we'd moved anyhow. Mama said it was an antique, that's why she kept it. Now she was rocking. She rocked and she cried.

"Get to bed," said Mason, and so I did, but I didn't sleep for a long time on account of Mama's rocking.

Once I saw an old movie about some coal miners. At the end of the movie one of the mines collapsed and all these men were trapped in the dark, waiting to be rescued. That's how I felt as I lay in my bed that night, listening to the rocking chair, listening to Mama, trying not to think about Daddy, like I was trapped and waiting, except I knew no one was coming to rescue us, not until they found Daddy.

Maybe they've found him.

Maybe not.

Is he hurt?

Is he scared?

Does he miss me?

The whole world had collapsed on top of me and just like those coal miners, I was cold and scared to death, afraid to move an inch. I wondered if I'd ever see the light again.

Chapter Nine

I woke up the next morning to the sound of hard rain against the window. The trees outside lashed back and forth in the wind. It was barely light out. Six-forty-five by the clock. Mason knocked on my door and said, "Get up," and I knew I hadn't dreamed any of the past couple of days.

We ate soup for breakfast. Mason looked troubled so I didn't ask him any questions. I took some soup up to Mama. She was snoring in the rocking chair with her mouth open. I didn't wake her up.

"How is she?" asked Mason when I got back downstairs.

"The same," I said.

"You go to school today," he said. "Tell them you were sick. You look sick. You should see yourself. They'll believe you for certain." His words stung, even though he hadn't meant to be mean. At least I didn't think he had.

"I have to have a note from Mama," I said.

"Write one yourself," said Mason. "You have good handwriting. Just don't act nervous when you give it to the teacher. No one will know." First it was lying on the phone. Now I'd be lying in a note. There wasn't any way around it.

"Are you going to take care of Mama?" I asked.

"'Course I will," he said. "I'll be here all day." Mason picked at a spot on the wall. He picked and picked. "Do you believe they'll find Daddy?" he whispered.

"Yes, I do," I said, "and real soon too." But did I think that? Was I lying to my own brother now? I knew what I wanted, but that didn't make it true. In my head, I wanted them to find Daddy and I knew if they could, they would. Did I believe they would find him? Down deep in my heart, did I believe it? I wasn't sure at all.

I didn't know what would happen to us next. That was the only truth I knew for sure.

"I know they'll find him, Mason," I told my brother. I didn't know what else to say.

Mason smiled and nodded. I pretended not to notice the tears welling up in his cat-green eyes.

When I got to school I felt like everyone was looking at me. I told myself it was pure imagination. I'd had family business I couldn't tell before. I'd learned that if I didn't say a word, people didn't find out. Like when we went to the foster home. We missed a day of school that time. The teacher didn't tell anyone else what happened and neither did Mama.

I took my phony note up to Mrs. Saunders. I'd had to write it six times before it looked grown-up. "You do look pale," she said, examining my face with her eyes. "Are you sure you're feeling better?" I nodded and was just about to turn around and go back to my desk when Mrs. Saunders said my name. "Bobbie Lynn." I turned around.

"I read in the paper that some men from our area are missing in action. Your dad isn't one of them, is he?" I froze and stared at her like a mule deer caught in the headlights of a truck. For a second I couldn't breathe.

I wanted to tell her.

Mrs. Saunders cared. She'd know what to do.

She'd tell the principal and he'd tell the police, and we'd be in a foster home by suppertime and Mama'd be—I didn't know where. I'd promised Daddy to take care of her. I couldn't tell. Not even Mrs. Saunders.

I stretched my mouth into a smile that hurt.

"Oh, no, ma'am," I said. "He's fine. It isn't him. No, not my dad." I giggled. It sounded awfully close to a choke but Mrs. Saunders didn't notice.

"Good," she said. "I was concerned about it."

Was I supposed to say something else? All I could do was nod. My face was blazing as I walked back to my desk. I saw Wendy out of the corner of my eye. She was staring right at me. So were thirty-two other pairs of eyes.

Wendy came and found me at recess. It had stopped raining and we had to go out. I told her right off that I didn't feel like playing. She said that was fine, but she didn't go away. I stood by the chainlink fence and looked out across the street. I wondered what Mason and Mama were up to. Who knows? Maybe Mama had snapped out of her delicate spell. Sometimes she did that. One day she'd be a mess, the next day she'd be herself again, but it usually happened when Daddy was on his way home.

Why hadn't they found him yet?

Wendy stood next to me without making a sound. It

74

gave me the creeps and it felt good at the same time. I thought about being at her house, whistling for those doves and feeling so happy, then feeling strange about the way she talked.

"Are you mad at me?" asked Wendy.

"No," I said. The other day, when I couldn't wait to get away from her, it was because all her questions, all her talk about angels, well, it made me plain jittery. I wasn't mad, but I sure didn't feel much like talking.

Had it really been only two days ago? I looked over at Wendy and she smiled. Her eyes matched the sky for color. I remembered what she'd said about everyone having an angel. No one in my family had one—that was for certain.

"Maybe you ought to go whistle or something," I said.

"Do you want me to go away?" she asked.

"Not if you don't want to," I said. "It's a free country."

"You're so sad," said Wendy.

"I don't care to talk about it," I said. I felt tears spring into my eyes.

"Okay," said Wendy.

A breeze fluttered my dress and made chicken skin come up on my legs. I wrapped my arms around myself. A lady across the street let a little black dog out into the yard. It lifted its leg on a bush. Behind me I heard voices chanting, "Red Rover, Red Rover, send Ronny right over," and then I heard laughter. The school bell rang and recess was over.

Wendy walked next to me into the school building. She walked so close that our arms bumped. How was it she could always put her finger on my feelings without me saying a single word? Could she read my mind? I told myself it was a foolish notion. Because right then I was wondering how long we could take care of Mama without anyone finding out what she'd done.

Up until that moment I'd told myself Mama was just extra upset, like the other times Daddy was gone, only now more so. Truth is, she really was worse than upset and I didn't know when it would end. Maybe Mama'd be sick a long time. Maybe they wouldn't find Daddy right away. Maybe Mama'd find that gun and go after God again.

Wendy was right. I was sadder than sad and scared to death. And I didn't dare to let her know it. By the time I got to Mrs. Saunders's classroom, I had chicken skin all the way up to my head.

When I got home that afternoon, Mason wasn't there. The back door was unlocked so I thought he must be around somewhere, but I looked all over and couldn't find him. I checked on Mama. She was asleep. A panicky feeling crept up my throat. Where was he? He said he'd watch her all day. Where could he be?

I spread my homework out on the table and stared at it. How was I supposed to care about Brazil and Venezuela when Daddy was missing in the jungle someplace and Mama was crying and sleeping all the time and now my brother was gone too? Two tears slipped off my nose and spilled on the page. One splashed in the Caribbean. The other missed my geography book completely. Mason came through the back door.

"Where have you been?" I yelled. I wiped my eyes so he wouldn't see I'd been crying, but before he could open his mouth I knew the answer to my own question. He had two grocery bags full of food, one in each arm.

"Simmer down and help put this food away," he said. He put the bags down on the kitchen counter.

"You said you'd stay home all day." I pulled out a half-gallon bottle of milk.

"I did," said Mason. "I only left when I knew you'd be coming home from school soon." He put some cans of chicken-noodle soup in the cupboard. "Mama just slept all day anyhow. It's not like she gets into any trouble."

"Did she eat anything?"

"Spaghetti and meatballs," he said. "Half the can."

"That's good," I said. "Eating's a good sign." I pulled a long loaf of Wonder bread out of one of the bags.

"Not good enough," said Mason. "She has to eat more than that."

"I'll make her some toast." I opened the bread and put two slices in the toaster. I heard Mason folding up the paper bags. I turned and looked at him. He had a big box of Velveeta in each hand.

"There's some apples and eggs and a box of corn flakes in that other bag. That's all the food I could buy," he said.

"I don't s'pose we'll need much more than that," I said. "Mama will be better soon." It had to be true. I willed it to be true. "Besides, she must have some other money someplace."

"She doesn't," said Mason.

"She has to," I said. I pushed the bread down.

"I said she doesn't," said Mason. "Are you too stupid to understand English?"

"I understand English just fine, Mr. Ugly. What about Daddy's paycheck?" I was sick of him bossing me around.

"It's all used up, plain and simple," said Mason. "Remember a few days back when Mama said paying rent and electric was going to clean us out until the next paycheck? This isn't a base, remember? How can you be so stupid?"

"Shut up, Mason!" I yelled back. "Daddy will send more—" My hand flew to my mouth. Mason looked away. The toast popped up. For a second it had smelled good. Now it smelled awful.

"If Mama doesn't get a whole lot better real soon," said Mason through clenched teeth, "we're in big trouble."

"It's not her fault, Mason," I said. "She can't help how she is."

"I know it," said Mason, and he simmered down some. "But remember what Daddy said that one time? Remember? About Mama's family?" I knew exactly what he was talking about but pretended not to. A few of Mama's relatives had had problems with nerves. I shook my head. I didn't want to think about it.

"Daddy said there was a weak streak in Mama's line." He pointed to his temple and tapped. "You know what happened to Uncle Louis."

"Don't talk about it," I snapped. "Mama doesn't allow it."

I turned my back on him. I put the toast on a plate and got out the Blue Bonnet and buttered it. I poured a glass of milk. Mama's oldest brother, Louis, was a drinker.

Daddy said he loved whiskey more than living. One night, when Mama was fifteen and Louis was around twenty-five or so, he went and drank himself to death. The worst part is, he had a wife and two babies. Daddy didn't know what happened to them. Mama's folks told everyone Louis died in an accident. I never even knew I'd had an uncle Louis until that day Daddy told me.

"I'm taking Mama something to eat," I said as calmly as I could. "She isn't crazy and she's nothing like Uncle Louis. She's delicate and that's different. You are just *shameful!* She's having a . . . a bad spell because of Daddy, that's all, and who wouldn't? And you're the one who's stupid. Mama needs love. She needs our help." My hands were shaking so badly some of the milk slopped out of the glass onto my wrist. How could Mason bring up Uncle Louis? Mama never drank. I put the food down and wiped my arm. "She'll get better if we take proper care of her so just quit all that crazy talk right now."

"I wish she'd hurry up and get well then," said Mason. "I don't want to be a nurse forever." He put one hand on his hip, stuck his chest out, and strutted across the kitchen with his rear end wagging. "How do I look?" he asked. "Do I make a good nurse?" He pretended to shake a thermometer and then he grabbed my wrist and checked my pulse. He said in a high voice, "My name is Nurse Mason. Open wide."

"No nurse could be so ugly," I said, and I couldn't help but smile. Mason can be such a smart aleck. Truth is, I didn't want to be a nurse forever either.

"I wish she'd get better too," I said. "Maybe we should call someone, maybe a doctor or something."

"Oh, there's a fine idea," said Mason. Now his voice was nasty. "Now *you* sound crazy. They'll lock her up for a hundred years for shooting that gun off. And they'll stick us who knows where. You want that?"

"No."

"There's no choice but to take care of her and try to get by until they find Daddy. They'd put Mama in the loony bin for sure if they knew how she is right now."

"Shut up!"

"What do you think Daddy would want? Huh? Would he want us to tell on her?" I clenched my teeth and didn't answer. How could my brother go from funny to mean in such a short time?

"I'm not talking to you anymore," I said, and carried the food out of the kitchen. I took deep breaths and squeezed my eyes tight against the tears that wanted to come. By the time I got to Mama's room I could hold the toast and glass of milk without trembling.

Mama was lying on her side, smoking a cigarette. The room was like a cave. "Hi," I said. "I brought you some toast."

"I'm not hungry," she muttered. Her breath was terrible and her hair was starting to look matted.

"You have to eat, Mama," I said. I sat beside her with the plate and glass in my hands. "Here's some milk too. You need it to feel better. That's what you always tell me. Try a little sip."

"No milk," she said, and then she coughed hard a few times. "Nothing helps," said Mama. "I want to sleep."

"Eat first," I said. "A little anyway, for me?" I waited for her to say something, to nod OK or shake her head no, anything, but she just stared. She didn't blink, she didn't move, she didn't even puff on her cigarette. I moved Mama's Bible over and set the plate and glass on her bedside table.

As soon as I was out the door she started to cry all over again.

The crying lasted an hour.

Mason pretended not to hear. He also pretended I was not in the room. How could he be so awful? He turned on the TV and watched *Gilligan's Island*. Mason turned it up so loud we could barely hear Mama. By the time the show was over, she was quiet.

I went to bed hungry, with my stomach in a hard ball, and I was half asleep when the phone rang. Who would call this time of night? Probably a wrong number. I heard Mason's door open and figured he'd get it. I heard him run down the stairs, and I heard him say hello and talk for a while. I heard him run back up the stairs but he didn't go to his own room. He stopped and opened my door. He switched on my light.

"Why'd you have to do that, Mason? You blinded me." I still felt mad at him. "Who was that on the phone, anyhow?"

"Aunt Jeri Lee."

I sat straight up.

Chapter Ten

"You liar," I said. I felt my heartbeat speed up.

"Swear to God it was her."

"Why would she call here?" I asked. "She knows how Mama feels."

"I know that," said Mason. He looked down and rubbed his foot against his leg.

"Well, what did she want?" Suddenly I was filled up with impatience. Why had Aunt Jeri Lee called? Why now? What had Mason told her?

"She says Daddy called her the day before he shipped out," said Mason. "He made her promise to call once a month and check up on us and she said she would whether Mama hung up on her or not. She was pretty happy I answered."

"That's the biggest bucket of hogwash I ever heard," I said. "Daddy wouldn't do that. He knows what Mama thinks of Aunt Jeri Lee."

"I'm only telling you what she told me," said Mason. "She wanted to know how everything's going."

"What did you say?" I had to know. "Tell me what you said." Mason looked up. He took forever to answer.

"Nothing."

"What do you mean? Speak plain."

"I told her everything was fine." I lay back down on my pillow and stared at the ceiling. Mason kept talking. "She wanted to know how Mama's taking it with Daddy being gone and all. I said fine. She said Matthew Mark tells everyone about his uncle Jimmy fighting the communists and that they're both real proud." Mason paused. "She wanted to know what all we'd heard from Daddy." I looked over at my brother. I could see he was fighting tears. "She didn't know. I could tell, Bobbie Lynn. She didn't know about him being MIA."

"Did you tell her?" I whispered.

"No," said Mason. "How could I?"

I didn't answer. I couldn't have done it either, tell Aunt Jeri Lee that her only brother was missing in action. Someone else should have to do that job, some grown-up person who does it all the time and doesn't care about the people he tells. Even if he did act big, Mason was just a kid. How could he tell her?

"Aunt Jeri Lee has a right to know about Daddy," I said.

"Then you call and tell her," snapped Mason. "She left her number. I wrote it on the chalkboard."

"I'm not calling her," I said, "so just settle down. Mama'd pitch a fit if I did and I don't want to anyhow. Where does Aunt Jeri Lee live anyway?"

"Austin."

"Did she say anything else?" I asked.

"She said call her if we need anything, and she'll call again next month. That's it." Mason rubbed his eyes.

"I'm going to bed." He switched off my light and closed the door and I was left alone in the dark with a heap of things to think about.

When Mason'd first said it was Aunt Jeri Lee on the phone a little tiny balloon of hope started to grow in my heart. I don't know why, now that I think about it. I mean, she was a complete stranger to us, not like a real aunt, the kind who knows you and brings your cousins over to play. Even so, for one split second I'd felt like there was a kind of thread between us, on account of us all being Brewers, but when Mason said she didn't know about Daddy and when he said he'd told her everything was fine, that thread broke clean in half. She didn't know anything. Just like everyone else.

Jeri Lee was on the outside. If she found out about Mama, she'd turn us in. What else could she do? Any grownup would do the same. And besides, there was real bad blood between Aunt Jeri Lee and my mama. Maybe Aunt Jeri Lee would be happy if Mama were locked up. Maybe she'd even feel like it was a kind of just desserts for Mama thinking she was trash.

If Aunt Jeri Lee had been a bad girl, maybe she was a bad grownup too. Maybe Mama never let us meet her for good reasons. Maybe it was Mama who was right about Aunt Jeri Lee, not Daddy.

She was going to call again in a month. She'd made Daddy a promise to check on us while he was gone. I'd made him a promise too, to give Mama all the extra TLC she needed while he was gone. How could I have known she'd need so much?

A month was a long, long time. By then the army

searchers would probably find Daddy. And then no one would have to give bad news to anyone else. As soon as they found Daddy, Mama'd snap out of it. I could hang on a while more. Next time Aunt Jeri Lee called, all we'd have was good news.

The next day was Saturday. I watched cartoons in between trying to get Mama to eat, listening to her carry on, and wishing I didn't have to go upstairs to her room. I looked for any little sign that this spell was coming to an end. It rained all day. In the afternoon, we watched a Tarzan film festival.

Mason and I didn't talk about Daddy and we didn't talk about the call from Aunt Jeri Lee. I thought about it though, every time I passed the telephone and saw her number up there on the little chalkboard.

It was a long day. Sunday wasn't much different.

On Sunday around suppertime I was making fried Velveeta sandwiches and Mason said, "When da grub runs out I'll have to pull another heist." He said it in a gangster accent, to sound funny. It only made me mad.

"No more stealing," I said. "I mean it."

"It's steal or starve," he said. "I spent all the money we had."

"A lady from the base called right after the news. She said she'd bring us dinner. Or maybe we could call Aunt Jeri Lee, tell her we're short on cash. She asked did we need anything. We could tell her Mama got the flu."

"NO!" said Mason. He grabbed me by the shoulders and shook hard. "We can't risk it. What could Aunt Jeri Lee do from clear down in Austin? If we made her suspicious she might call the police and have them check on us. They'd lock Mama up for sure. We are going to do whatever we have to do until Mama is better. We're going to act normal, get it? N-O-R-M-A-L." I pushed his hands away and tried to hit him but he ducked in time and jumped back.

"Maybe they wouldn't put us in a foster home," I said. "You don't know everything."

"It's worse than that," he said. "We aren't in Texas anymore, Bobbie Lynn."

"So what?"

"So in this town kids don't go to foster homes. They go to juvenile hall."

"Even if they aren't bad?" Mason nodded and lowered his voice.

"I was talking to a kid named Ricky. He said he's been in the juvie before, for shoplifting." I stared at Mason but he looked away and ignored me. "Ricky said it's not just bad kids, it's all kinds of kids, orphans and everything, all in one big place. They call it a children's home, but it's not a home. It's jail with bars on the windows and all. Want to go to jail?"

"You never told me this before," I said.

"I didn't want to scare you." Upstairs, I heard Mama get out of bed and then the rocking began. She moaned and rocked. Mason and I stood there listening, not making a sound.

"I'll check on her this time," said Mason. "And no

telling anyone about the food situation. Unless you like the thought of jail." He looked up toward Mama and then he looked at me. "Because, Bobbie Lynn, there's no one to get us out if they lock us up."

Mama only cried for twenty minutes and then she fell asleep in the rocking chair. It was a relief. I'd expected her to rock and cry for hours. I filled the bathtub with hot water and tried to get warm but it didn't work. I lay with the water all the way to my chin and shivered like a wet dog.

I knew one thing was certain. Jail would be a whole lot worse than this. And what would they do to Mama in a place for crazy people? Probably tie her up and give her shocks. I saw it in a movie. Poor Mama, all scared and trapped in a strange, horrible place like that with all sorts of torment going on. We couldn't let it happen. She needed us too much. I ran some more hot water but it didn't work. Nothing could get me warm.

Chapter Eleven

Monday morning Mason said I could go to school. I didn't argue with him. "Make sure she eats something," I said.

"You know I will," he replied. Mason never did like school much. Now he had a good excuse to stay home. He could take care of Mama as well as I could. That's what I told myself when I started feeling guilty about leaving her.

I didn't remember about the geography homework until Mrs. Saunders asked for it. She came by each person's desk and stood there waiting with her hand out and a big smile on her face. I stared at my hands. My nails needed clipping. I curled my fingers so no one else would see. Mrs. Saunders had on bright red shoes. "Homework, Bobbie Lynn?"

"I forgot," I said, and heard some of the kids snickering. I heard someone mimic my accent.

"Ah fergot."

Just then my stomach let out a big growl. Mrs. Saunders put her hand under my chin and made me look up. "You still don't look well, Bobbie Lynn," she said quietly. "Were you sick this weekend?"

"No, ma'am," I said. "I don't have any excuses for the homework." Mrs. Saunders had on big red earrings that matched her shoes. Her glasses had slid down her nose a bit and it made her eyes look small.

"Are you getting enough sleep?" It felt like my ears were burning up, because I knew every single kid in the room was staring at me.

"Yes, ma'am," I said. "My mother is strict about bedtime."

"All right then," she said. "You can turn it in tomorrow, but you'll have to take a lower grade for being late. I was clear about that on Friday."

"Yes, ma'am, I know," I said, looking at my hands again and wishing Mrs. Saunders would leave me alone. The red shoes moved away. I tried to be the most unnoticeable girl in the whole class for the rest of the morning.

Wendy sat across from me at the lunch table. "What did you do this weekend?" she asked. She opened her lunch sack and pulled out a peanut butter and jelly sandwich on brown bread. The waxed-paper bag crinkled when she opened it. My mouth watered.

"Watched TV mostly," I said, hoping she wouldn't ask a lot of snoopy questions. Mason's words echoed in my head: *Normal. N-O-R-M-A-L.*

"Us too, because of all the rain," she said. She'd bought a carton of milk and now she stuck the straw in the opening. "Did you watch *The Monkees* on Saturday?" I nodded. "Davy is so cool," said Wendy.

I opened my own sack. I'd made a little sandwich with the heel of the Wonder bread loaf and some deviled ham. I took a bite.

"You aren't on a diet, are you?" asked Wendy. Her mouth was full of sandwich. She took a drink of milk and washed it down.

"No," I said. "Not really."

"You aren't that fat, you know," said Wendy. "You're just sturdy." I felt myself blush. Wendy kept talking. "I wish I was sturdier," she said. "No one ever thinks I'm twelve. I eat all the time and it doesn't help." Now she pulled a waxed-paper bag of vanilla wafers out of her lunch sack. "Want some?" she asked.

I'd finished my half-sandwich and I was still hungry. "Thanks," I said, and took one. When I looked up Wendy was staring at my face. She had a serious look and it made me feel nervous.

"My problem is," she said, "I get full too fast. Like a bird. Eat, eat, eat, all day long, but only one worm at a time." She giggled and pushed the rest of the cookies across to me. "Want these? Otherwise I'm going to throw them away."

"That'd be a shame," I said. Wendy jumped up from her seat.

"I want some more milk," said Wendy. She dug a nickel out of her jumper pocket and showed it to me. "Be right back." She ran off to the lunch line and came back with another carton of milk. "What else did you do this weekend, besides watching *The Monkees*?"

I ate another cookie. How could a dry old vanilla wafer taste so good? Chewing bought me some time to think. Wendy stuck the straw in her milk and took a sip. I swallowed. Time for more lies, I thought. I didn't want to lie to Wendy. I don't know why, but somehow it felt worse to lie to her than to Mrs. Saunders or Mama's boss.

"My mother is feeling poorly," I said slowly, rolling the last cookie in my fingers. "So I stuck close to home. She has the flu." It was only barely a lie at all. I put another cookie in my mouth.

"Last time my mom had the flu it turned out to be Therese," said Wendy with a big grin. "Is your mom P.G.?"

"No," I said. "It isn't that."

"How many kids in your family, anyway?"

"Two," I said. "Me and my big brother, Mason. He's thirteen."

"So when will your dad be back?" asked Wendy. *Maybe never*, I thought, and a sickening chill ran up my spine all the way to my scalp. I shrugged and didn't look at her. "A tour lasts a year, give or take."

"That's a long time to be away," said Wendy. "Know what? I can't drink another drop of this milk." She pulled a clean straw out of her jumper pocket and stuck it in the hole. "Hurry up and finish it or the lunch ladies will yell at us for throwing milk away." The lunch recess bell rang. "You don't want me to get detention, do you?" I shook my head and sucked down the milk. Wendy watched until she heard my slurp at the bottom of the carton. I crushed the milk carton and put it in my sack. "Thanks," said Wendy. "I never could have finished it. Want to swing?"

We waited until there were two swings side by side. Then we had a contest to see who could swing the highest. I went faster because my legs are longer, but Wendy went higher because she's so light. For a few minutes every single bad thing in my life went away as I swung back and forth, trying hard to get as high as Wendy.

"It's almost like flying," said Wendy.

"Yeah, it is," I said. But thinking of flying made me think of airplanes, and thinking about airplanes made me think of Daddy, shot down, missing, hurt, and then I was tired of swinging. The recess bell rang and we went inside. Wendy said we should swing again and I said, "That'd be nice," but I didn't mean it.

The bell rang at three o'clock and Mrs. Saunders dismissed us. Wendy caught up to me on my way to the lockers. "Want to come over tomorrow?"

"I don't know," I said. I opened my locker and took out my sweater.

"I always take Jean for a drive on Tuesdays," she said. I must have looked surprised because Wendy giggled and said, "Not in the car, in her wheelchair. I have to steer, so I call it going for a drive."

"It'll depend on how my mom is feeling," I said. That much was the truth. Wendy's locker was five down from mine. She opened hers and pulled out a green jacket with a hood.

"We have to get Jean out of the house on Tuesdays between four and four-thirty," said Wendy. "My mom started taking piano lessons this year"—she slammed her locker shut with a bang—"and Jean sings so loud it drives the teacher batty." Wendy came and stood next to me. She barely reached my shoulder. "The piano teacher is about eighty years old. She's not used to Jean."

"I never heard of a grownup taking piano lessons," I said.

"My dad gave it to Mom for her birthday. She always wanted to learn." Wendy tiptoed up and whispered in my ear. "So far she's terrible, but we tell her we like it." I smiled to think of plump little Mrs. Feeney taking piano lessons.

We walked down the hall to the back doors and went out to cut across the playground. "I'll ask," I said, which was a lie because Mama was in no condition to be asked anything.

"You could have dinner," said Wendy, flipping back a curl which had escaped from her messy ponytail. "We're eating early this week because Dad is on evenings, you know, five to one."

I heard Debbie's voice behind us. "Weeny," called Debbie, "tell Ellie Mae she's blocking the view of the playground."

Wendy whirled around.

"Shut your face, you *insect*," she yelled. "You stinking stinkbug!" Debbie's mouth snapped open and shut. In a flash Wendy stooped down and filled her hand with gravel. "Here's a close-up of the playground. Want to see?" she yelled. "I dare you." Debbie put her nose in the air and walked past quickly. Her friends whispered among themselves. Wendy dropped the gravel, wiped her hand on her jumper skirt, and spun back around to face me. She was breathless with fury. "I hope your mom lets you come over. Jean would like it." Her face was flushed and her freckles were bright. Her eyes were wild.

"Insect?" I asked, squeaking out the word.

"I couldn't think of anything better," said Wendy. She looked over her shoulder. "DOG POOP!" she screamed. Some kids stared. I hoped no teachers had heard. Saying "dog poop" was the same as cursing.

Wendy picked a tiny bit of gravel from under her thumbnail with her teeth and spit it out. "Do you want my mom to call your mom?" she asked.

"No!" I said, way too quickly. "She doesn't need to bother." Wendy gave me a strange look. I swallowed hard and forced myself to smile. *Normal*, I told myself. "Give me your phone number and I'll call you when I know if I can come over or not, okay?"

"Groovy," said Wendy. She dug in her book bag and pulled out a blue ballpoint pen. She clicked it open and handed it to me. "Just write on your hand," she said. "Our number is simple to remember. The last part is the date of Christmas. The first part, Broadway, is the street Sears is on downtown. Sears is where the Christmas catalog comes from, right? So it's BR4, four for the four kids my mom and dad have to buy presents for. BR4-1225. Get it?"

"I think so," I said. I could see why kids thought she was strange. I said good-bye and we went our separate ways. When she was half a block away, Wendy turned around and yelled.

"Call before eight or I'll be in the tub!" I waved and nodded and headed toward my house.

* * *

Mason was sprawled on the couch watching *General Hospital*. He was facing down and all I could see was one eye looking up at me. He needed a haircut. His hair was way past the back of his collar.

"Guess what?" he said without moving. "Bart has brain cancer."

"Bart who?" I asked.

"The guy on *General Hospital*. He'll probably be dead by Friday. It's real sad." Mason flopped over on his back, put his feet and arms in the air like a dead sheep, and let his tongue hang out. "I'm dyin', Miz Bobbie Lynn. I got brain cancer from too much bad TV."

"You're too stupid to live," I said, but I couldn't help smiling. He started to choke and gag like he was dying, until I grabbed a pillow off the easy chair and threw it at his head and asked, "How's Mama?" Mason sat up. His hair was an awful mess, but where would we get fifty cents for a haircut?

"She woke up a while ago and asked for her cigarettes," said Mason. "I found three more packs in her drawer." He paused and picked at a spot of dirt on the sofa. "She asked if Daddy had called yet."

"What did you tell her?" I asked. I sat down in the easy chair and we looked at each other for what felt like a long time.

"I told her Daddy called when she was sleeping and that he told me not to wake her up. I told her he'd call back next week."

"You *lied* to her?" I said. "Right to her face? Now she's going to think he's going to call and what if they don't—"

95

"It worked, didn't it?" snapped Mason. "She went right back to sleep. And he is coming back." He set his jaw and looked defiantly at me. His look was like a dare. *I dare you to say he's not coming back.*

"You have no right to lie to her about Daddy," I said. "It's cruel."

"She's acting kookie, Bobbie Lynn. What was I supposed to do?"

"Shut up," I said, but it came out sounding pretty tired.

"You got any better ideas, you just let me know," said Mason.

I left Mason without replying and went into the kitchen. We had six potatoes. I peeled two big ones and put them in a pan of water to boil. I thought about the sky-high pan of potatoes Wendy and I had peeled, and remembered her invitation.

I left the kitchen and went up to Mama's room, taking the stairs two at a time. I opened the door without knocking first. Mama was propped up on two pillows, but her eyes were closed. She didn't notice me at all until I spoke. Then all she did was turn her head slightly in my direction.

"Mama?" I said, "I'm fixing potatoes for dinner. You want some?" Mama shook her head.

"Toast," she said, and blinked twice, real slowly.

"We're out of bread," I said.

"Not hungry."

"I am," I said. "And so is Mason." I tried to keep the fear out of my voice. I tried to sound cheerful but it didn't come out that way. We were going to get a lot hungrier when the food ran out. "If I bring you a little supper, will you try?"

Mama's eyes were closed. I crossed over to her bedside and picked up her hand. It was hot and dry. I squatted down so my face was level with hers.

"Do you need anything?" I asked, but Mama had fallen asleep or wasn't listening, or maybe she just didn't feel like answering, because she didn't move or make a sound. I put her hand under the blankets and covered her up. I took a deep breath and held back the tears. "I love you, Mama," I whispered. I kissed her on the forehead. "Please get better."

Do you need anything? My words to Mama echoed in my brain. Did I need anything? 'Course I did. Like food, like Mama well again, like Daddy—I made myself stop thinking and went downstairs. Mason was still on the couch. Daffy Duck was chasing a little outer-space man around a palm tree.

Mason and I ate mashed potatoes without talking. After dinner I did the dishes. Mason took Mama some mashed potatoes and then he said he had to go somewhere. "You could at least dry these dishes," I said.

"Not my week," he said, and before I could kick him he slipped out the back door. By the time I got to the back door, he was already in the garage.

"Where do you think you're going?"

"None of your beeswax," he said. He rode his bike out of the garage and pulled the heavy door down to close it. I didn't want to be left alone with Mama. What if she asked about Daddy?

"Stay home, Mason. Please?"

"Can't," he said. "I have something to do." He rode off down the street and I was left there standing in the door with a dishrag in my hand and a burning, sick feeling in my stomach. *Stop being such a baby*, I told myself. Mason had been home all day with Mama. I could manage awhile. On my way back to the sink I looked up at the paper patches on the ceiling. The masking tape was peeling in one spot. I'd have to fix it later.

I finished the dishes and went up to Mama's room. The potatoes were untouched. I shook Mama's shoulder. "Mama?" I said quietly. She groaned and turned toward me. "Sit up and try to eat, Sweetie Pie." She looked at me like I was talking Chinese or something. "Please sit up," I said. I helped pull her up. I sat on the bed next to her and took the plate of potatoes in one hand and the fork in the other. "You have to eat," I said. I picked up a mouthful of potatoes on the fork. "Open." Mama opened her mouth and I put the food in. Just like that. After she swallowed it she smiled.

I did it again. "Open," I said, and she did, and I fed her the whole pile that way. Then I got her some water and put the glass to her lips. "Drink this." I had to hold the glass for her. She didn't even try to hold it herself, but she drank it all that way and I didn't spill much.

I wiped her lips with a Kleenex because I'd forgotten to bring up a napkin. Then I got the idea to wash her whole face. I hadn't even thought about it. Mama hadn't washed or had a bath for who knows how many days. I felt mad at myself for forgetting. I got a washcloth and soap and washed her face and hands. She seemed to doze off and on. When I was done I dried her face. "Get well real soon, Mama," I whispered, and then I left her room.

As I shut the door she started to cry.

How long could we go like this? I sat on the top step with my face in my hands. They smelled like Ivory soap. My legs started to shake so I hugged them tight, but that didn't do any good and soon I was shaking all over.

All Mama's carrying on made it feel like we were living in a haunted house. No, it was worse than that, because ghosts are dead. They don't need anyone to take care of them. Ghosts don't have to be fed and washed.

Was Daddy a ghost now?

If Daddy was a ghost, could he see us here? Could he hear Mama crying? Could he see how hard me and Mason were trying to take care of her? If Mama got a breakdown from not knowing whether Daddy was alive or dead, did that mean it could happen to me? Was the weakness in Mama's line part of me too?

I stood up and stretched my legs. Then I went back into Mama's room. I shut the door and sat in the dark with her. I sat in the middle of the floor. At first I just listened to her sadness. I hadn't wanted to hear it before. I'd shut it out, turned up the TV, and plugged my ears. I'd hated the sound of her sadness and wished she'd be quiet. Now I heard it. I listened. I let myself feel some of it with her. Mama's sadness fed my own.

"Shhh, shhh, shhh," I said, and I rocked myself back and forth. "Shhh, Mama, shhh."

Mama spoke. "Jimmy called today but I didn't get to talk to him. Did you talk to him?"

"No, Mama," I said. "Not today." I choked on the words.

"In the winter it's real cold in Korea."

"Korea?" I didn't mean to say it out loud but I did. "Daddy's in Viet—" Mama interrupted me.

"Why doesn't he call me, Mama?" she said to me.

Did she think I was Grandmamma? *Her* mama? My heart raced at top speed and my mouth felt dry as leather. Should I turn a light on so she could see it was me?

"It's long distance," I said. "Calls across the ocean cost a pile of money." Mama whimpered and I said, "Shhh."

"I just can't do without him," she said. "I miss him. I miss him."

"Me too," I said. I got up and went over to the bed and lay down beside Mama. I put my arms around her. "Hush now, Mama," I said. "Try to be brave." And then I started to sing.

> *Hush little baby, don't say a word.*
> *Papa's gonna buy you a mockingbird.*
> *If that mockingbird don't sing*
> *Papa's gonna buy you a diamond ring.*

Daddy sang it to me when I stubbed my toe and when Mason broke my Tinker Toy house and when I fell off my bike and got dirt in my chin.

> *If that diamond ring turns brass*
> *Papa's gonna buy you a looking glass.*

He sang it when I had chicken pox. He sang it when

Miz Winfred's dog, Samson, ate all my new crayons except for Goldenrod Yellow.

> If that looking glass gets broke,
> Papa's gonna buy you a billy goat.
> If that billy goat runs away—

I stopped at the part about running away. I couldn't remember how it ends, what happens to the billy goat or how the papa in the song makes the baby happy in the end. So I hummed it awhile without the words and by the time I was done, Mama was quiet. I wiped the tears off my cheeks and leaned over to kiss her head. Then I got up and tiptoed out, closing the door softly behind me.

Mama'd thought I was her mama. She'd thought Daddy was in Korea, not Vietnam. How could she be so confused? Daddy was gone and so was Mama. I hoped like anything that they would both come home.

The screen door slammed and Mason came in whistling the theme song from *Gilligan's Island*.

"Come and get it," he yelled. I went downstairs to the kitchen. Mason had a half-gallon of chocolate ice cream open on the counter and a big spoon in one hand.

"Where did you get that?" I asked.

"I bought it," he said, and then he pulled a dollar out of his pocket and waved it under my nose.

"Where did you get that money," I asked, scared of the

answer but too tired to make a fuss. Stealing a little food was one thing. Stealing money, somehow that was way, way worse.

"It's mine," he said.

"I said where'd you get it, Mason."

"Bottles," he said. "I was down in the basement today and got the idea to take back all the soda-pop bottles we have down there."

"There weren't probably even a dozen," I said.

"On my way to the store I figured I could go to the neighbors too."

"You went begging for bottles?"

"No, stupid. I told them I was doing a project for school, a survey. I said I was doing percentages, you know, so many green, so many clear."

"And they gave you all their bottles? Just like that?"

"After I counted them I offered to get rid of them. Like this." Mason straightened up and grinned. When he spoke it was in the most exaggerated backwoods accent I'd ever heard. "Why, ma'am, I sure do thank you for lettin' me count these here bottles. You did me a big old favor and if there's anythang I can do for you folks, y'all let me know." He stopped to listen, as though someone were talking to him. "Yes, ma'am, I'm from the South. Born in Georgia. That's where my people come from. My daddy's over fighting the communists in Vietnam." Mason looked down. "I sure do miss him." Mason looked up and said in a whisper, "Here's where I kept my head down and stood there looking pitiful. Then I said, 'Ma'am, if you'd like, I could haul these bottles off fer ya.'"

I giggled at my big brother. "Did they all give you bottles?"

"I had to make five trips to the corner store." Mason unfolded the money. "I got three dollars and eighty-five cents. There's some food in the sack over there on the floor." Mason pointed with his chin. "I thought you could put everything away, since you didn't do any of the hard work."

"First," I said, digging in with my spoon, "I want ice cream." We ate half the carton and put the rest away.

"Mama okay?" asked Mason, wiping his mouth on his sleeve.

"Sleeping for now," I said. I didn't have the nerve to tell him how mixed up she'd been.

"I'm going to watch TV," said Mason. And then he belched.

"You're a hog," I said.

"And you're too ugly," he replied. I swung at his head but he ducked and then he ran into the living room.

I unpacked the groceries. One jar of Tang, one loaf of bread, a box of corn flakes, milk, eggs, and at the very bottom, a long, black licorice whip.

I'm the only one in the family who likes black licorice. I put the food away and bit the inside of my cheek because an awful lot of feelings were oozing up just then, like deep mud between bare toes. I went in and sat down next to Mason. I bit into my licorice rope. "Bobbie Lynn!" said Mason. "Get that stinking thing away from me. I hate that smell and you know it." This time, I didn't miss. I whacked him right over the head with the licorice.

Chapter Twelve

I forgot I was supposed to call Wendy until the phone rang the next morning. I'd just finished the late geography homework and was mixing up some Tang to take to Mama, along with some scrambled eggs. I set the glass down with the spoon still in it and picked up the phone. Wendy's phone number was still on the palm of my hand.

It was Mr. Blake, Mama's new boss at the Piggly Wiggly. I listened to him talk.

"All right. I'll let her know," I said. "Good-bye."

"Well?" said Mason.

"He said Mama has to be back at work by Wednesday or he'll have to give the job to someone else."

"That's tomorrow," said Mason. "Wednesday's tomorrow."

"He said a week was all he could give her, sick or not."

"She won't be able to go back tomorrow," said Mason. He flopped down into a chair and stuffed a piece of bread into his mouth without toasting it. I waited for him to finish chewing. My eyes automatically turned up and looked at the ceiling Mama had blown to bits.

"What are we going to do?" I asked.

"How do I know?" said Mason with a big sigh. "Do I look like a grownup to you?"

Right then he looked more like a little boy than usual. His hair needed a trim and his shirt was wrinkled. One shirttail hung out of his jeans. He took a drink of Tang. "I don't want to stay home," said Mason. "I don't think Mama needs a baby sitter. Maybe we should let her alone. Maybe we're making her worse by doing everything for her. What do you think about that?"

"I think you're crazy, that's what." We stared at each other for a second. Then Mason turned away and looked in the refrigerator. "I'll stay home today," I said. I could still call Wendy, tell her I couldn't come. I felt a big twinge of disappointment inside.

"No, don't do that," said Mason. "Normal, remember?" I nodded. "I have this plan. What if we make Mama some bread and butter, maybe leave her some Tang and tell her there's food downstairs if she needs it, and maybe she'll have the gumption to feed herself. Maybe it would even help her get better, you know, doing a few things herself. Maybe we're babying her too much."

Could Mason be right? Were we doing all the wrong things?

"I had to feed her last night, Mason," I said. "Bite by bite." Mason pointed at the eggs and Tang I'd made for Mama.

"Take the food up and see how she's doing this morning."

"Someone has to stay home," I said, wishing Mason was right but feeling guilty at the same time. Mama needed so much TLC. I couldn't let her down. I'd promised Daddy. But what if taking care of her meant letting her do something for herself?

"Morning, Mama. Here's some breakfast," I said, wondering if she remembered last night at all. "Can you eat?" At first I wasn't sure if she'd heard me.

"Let me sleep," said Mama finally. Her voice was like a croak more than a regular voice.

All Mama wanted to do during the day was sleep. Maybe Mason was right. Maybe if we left her some food she'd be fine until we came home. It was nighttime that she was so bad off, not daytime. Maybe she didn't need us as much as we thought.

"Mason and me gotta go back to school today," I said. Did Mama hear me? She didn't open her eyes. "That okay with you? Could you manage all right without us, just until school's out?" I thought I saw her nod her head.

"Okay," I said, and started for the door. "You sure you don't need anything?"

"Did I get a letter?" Her voice was weak and sounded so pitiful I had to look away. My pretty Mama. She was nothing but a wreck now.

"Not today," I said, trying to sound hopeful but not doing a very good job of it. "Maybe tomorrow, though." It was so easy to lie. Too easy. How could I tell her the truth?

I closed her door and went downstairs. Maybe Mason was right. Maybe it was worth a try. He was still sitting at the kitchen table. "Well?" he said.

"Better write yourself a note," I said. "We're going to school."

Mason said he'd come home to check on Mama at lunch time. Then he got his bike out of the garage and rode to school instead of walking. I told him about Wendy's invitation. I thought he'd say I couldn't go, but he didn't. "Stop home before you go," said Mason. "If Mama's fine, go on to your friend's house. And don't tell anybody anything, hear?"

"Don't forget to write a note," I said.

"I'm gonna say I had typhoid fever," said Mason, and then he left out the back door. I heard the garage door go up. I ran upstairs and brushed my teeth. I poked my head in Mama's door on the way by.

"We're going to school, Mama." I heard her murmur in reply. "Mason will come home at noon to check on you." She didn't say anything. I felt a big pile of guilt over leaving her, but it seemed like the right thing to do. I waited for her to say "don't go," but she didn't. She just slept. She'd sleep all day. At least that's what I hoped.

Wendy waved at me from the front row of our classroom, but I didn't get a chance to talk to her until morning recess. It was raining so we all had to play in the gym. It was so noisy that Wendy had to shout for me to hear her.

"How come you didn't call?" she asked.

"I forgot until after eight," I said, "and you said not to call after eight."

"Can you come over?"

"Maybe," I said. "Probably. I have to run by my house and check on something first."

"Oh, that's okay," said Wendy. "We're going to have so

much fun with Jean!" She grabbed both my hands and squeezed. I pulled away.

"Let's get a drink," I said, heading for the drinking fountain. Wendy followed behind me.

"I hope it quits raining or we won't be able to take Jean for her drive," she said. "But even if we can't, you can still come over and play, and have dinner. Mom's fixing fried chicken. It was my idea. I said you'd probably like it since you're from the South. Do you like fried chicken?" I took a drink from the water fountain.

"I do," I said.

"Me too," said Wendy, "even though I'm a Yankee from Pittsburgh."

I turned in my geography lesson right after recess. Mrs. Saunders said it looked fine. We did division until noon. Wendy and I sat together at lunch. She said she didn't like Oreo cookies so she gave them all to me. Debbie called me a whale. Wendy wadded her lunch sack into a ball and threw it at Debbie's head and the lunch lady saw her so she had to sit outside the principal's office instead of playing. I sat with her, even though I wasn't in trouble.

"You should ignore Debbie when she teases," I said.

"I never ignore mean people," said Wendy. "They should learn they can't pick on someone just because she's small."

Or big. "Thanks," I said, and Wendy's scowl turned into a big grin. No one had ever gotten in hot water on my account before. I felt bad for her, sitting out recess and what all, but I felt good too. I was proud to sit with her.

We sat there until the bell rang. Wendy got a lecture from the principal's secretary and then we went back to our class. "Meet you at the lockers after school," said Wendy. Then she hurried to her desk and slid into her chair just as the second bell rang.

Around two o'clock it stopped raining. By three the sun was shining. Wendy and I started out with sweaters on, but halfway across the playground we took them off. "Great weather for a drive," said Wendy. Her legs were so short she had to take extra steps to keep up with me. Debbie and company were nowhere in sight. That lunch sack did its job. I wished I had half a pinch of Wendy's gumption. I thought maybe some of it would rub off on me if we spent time together. Then I remembered Wendy saying they were moving back to Pittsburgh. Stevie had said they weren't. Why did Wendy seem so sure?

I told her I had to stop by my house. I was nervous thinking she might ask to come along, but she didn't.

"I'll meet you at my house in a few minutes, okay?" she said. "I'm supposed to come right home and help." I let out a silent sigh of relief. I didn't want Wendy asking questions. I didn't want to have to lie.

There was a note from Mason on the kitchen table. "Everything A-OK at noon. Mom ate toast and an apple for lunch, plus all the breakfast." I ran upstairs and looked in on Mama. She was sleeping. The glass of Tang was empty and so was the plate of scrambled eggs and for once I felt a little twinge of hopefulness. Eating is always a good sign when someone's been sickly. Leave it to Mason not to take the dirty dishes downstairs, I thought, and it made me smile. Mason's such a pig.

I reached down and patted Mama's shoulder. She seemed peaceful enough. She'd be just fine. I could wake her, I told myself. But why bother her? She'd tell me to go on to Wendy's if she knew I wanted to go. I felt a little guilty leaving, but something inside made me want to leave more than I thought I should stay.

Besides, Mason would be home any time now. Mama'd only be alone for a few more minutes. I picked the dirty dishes up, took them down to the sink, and left for Wendy's house.

Chapter Thirteen

Stevie answered the door when I knocked. "Three-thirteen," he said. "Dinner's at three-thirty."

"Hey," I said. "How are you, Stevie?"

"Hungry," he said, and opened the door. "Wendy says everyone from the South eats fried chicken. How many pieces can you eat?"

"Shut up, Stevie," said Wendy, "and help finish setting the table."

"Katie, don't say 'shut up,'" called Mrs. Feeney from the kitchen. Therese was in a highchair by the dining-room table. She was eating Cheerios one by one. Right next to her sat a thin man with a bald head. He had only a fringe of red hair and a whole lot of freckles, even on his head. I figured it must be Wendy's dad. He didn't see me at first because he had Jean on his lap and was trying to feed her. She sprawled across his legs. Her chest was covered with a very large white bib. "Come on, Jeannie girl," said Mr. Feeney. "Open up now."

"Dad, this is Bobbie Lynn," said Wendy. She grabbed my hand and pulled me over to the table.

"Pleased to meet you, sir," I said.

"Nice to meet you too," said Mr. Feeney. Wendy pointed at Jean.

"Hey, Jean," I said.

"Who's that, Jean?" asked Wendy. "Who is that, Jean?" She took my hand and put it on Jean's tiny hand. "It's Bobbie Lynn!"

"It's me again," I said. Jean swung her head in my direction.

"Wah," she said.

"That's 'hi,'" said Wendy.

"No, it's baby talk," said Stevie.

"You are a total imbecile," said Wendy.

"Katie, watch the tongue," said Mr. Feeney with a frown.

"You should pay Mom and Dad to call you Wendy too," said Stevie. "Otherwise you're still Katie."

"I should pay you to go soak your head," said Wendy.

"Kate!" said Mr. Feeney. He spooned some mashed potatoes into Jean's mouth and then he smiled down at her. "Chew, Jeannie girl." He took Jean's jaw in one hand and made the chewing motion. She caught on and chewed a little. Then he stroked her neck. "Now swallow. That's it." I'd never seen anyone feed such a big kid. It made me think of feeding Mama. I hoped she was well enough to eat all on her own from here on. Jean wasn't exactly big, but she wasn't a baby either. Would someone always have to feed her like this?

"She chokes a lot," said Wendy, who must have noticed how I was staring. "Then she spits all over the place so keep out of the danger zone. Dad, Bobbie Lynn is from Texas. She saw a rattlesnake once."

"Only a dead one, sir," I said, hoping Mr. Feeney wouldn't ask me as many questions as Wendy had. He put some more mashed potatoes on a spoon.

"Glad you could join us," he said.

Dinner was a bit on the noisy side, except for Mr. Feeney, who didn't say much. Mostly he helped Jean eat and drink, and he wiped her face a lot. He finished eating and carried Jean over to her wheelchair. He strapped her upright and came back to eat his own meal. Jean was quiet as a mouse.

Mrs. Feeney wanted to know if her fried chicken was just right. I said it was perfect and she grinned so hard her chubby cheeks looked like pink balls. Wendy and Mrs. Feeney tore Therese's food into little pieces and put it on her tray. She ate with her hands and made a lot of noise. Stevie cut all his food into squares, even the mashed potatoes. I ate until I was stuffed as a Thanksgiving turkey. I can't remember when food tasted so good. I couldn't remember the last time Mama had fixed a big dinner, either.

At four o'clock Mr. Feeney said he had to leave for work. Mrs. Feeney jumped up and started clearing the dishes. "The piano teacher will be here at four-fifteen," said Wendy as she cleaned up Therese's tray and wiped her face with a washcloth. "Let's get going." I thanked Mrs. Feeney for dinner, but she was so busy cleaning and clearing that I'm not sure she heard me. Wendy wheeled Jean into a side room and said, "I'll be back in a second." In a few minutes they came back out. "Had to change her diaper," whispered Wendy. "It sure is a good thing she's stayed so little. Want to help with her sweater?"

It hadn't dawned on me until just then that Jean wore a diaper. Wendy talked about changing it like she was talking about changing shoes and socks. Jean would need someone to change her and feed her all her life. It had to be a lot of work but none of the Feeneys seemed to mind. And they didn't seem embarrassed or ashamed of Jean, either. I thought about the retarded boy I'd seen way back when. Maybe his family loved him this much. Maybe that's why they took him to parades and let him yell.

We got Jean bundled up and strapped tight in her chair again and were wheeling her down the ramp just as the front doorbell rang. "That's the music teacher," said Wendy. "Bye, Mom. Have a good lesson," she yelled.

Wendy pushed Jean's chair around to the front of the house and we started down the sidewalk. "Where do you go most days?" I asked.

"Well, when Stevie comes we go to the park so he can feed the ducks. He likes to count them. I swing on the swings, Stevie feeds ducks, and Jean squeals when the ducks quack. Want to go there?"

"Sure," I said. I looked over at Jean. Her blue eyes were opened wide. She was sort of hunched over, but the strap around her chest kept her sitting. I guessed she couldn't sit up herself. All of a sudden I thought of Daddy. If they found him, if he weren't dead, he could be wounded, and maybe he'd be in a wheelchair too. Who'd take care of him? Surely Mama couldn't do it. Would a grown-up man need diapers?

I remembered Mama's old beau, the officer who'd lost his legs. Mama wouldn't have done too good with a husband who needed nursing. Maybe that's why they didn't marry. She needed someone strong like Daddy. Thinking about Daddy got me thinking about shooting and blood and hospitals and Mama calling me "Mama" and I wished I could make those thoughts go away.

Wendy chattered as we walked, but I didn't hear what she said. Up until then I'd made all my scared feelings about Daddy stop, like when you plug up the sink and the water stops going down. The water just sits there and gets cold. Was he dead? No one knew. Was he alive? Was he hurt? Did he miss me? I missed him, and as soon as I let myself think that, I made the feelings that came with it stop, like the plug in the sink. It wasn't safe to think about Daddy. Not even a little.

"See how she listens to everything?" I heard Wendy say. I looked over at Jean. The breeze blew her curly hair around her face. She cocked her head this way and that, listening to Wendy, listening to everything.

"Bub," said Jean.

"No," said Wendy. "There aren't any birds around." She turned to me. "That's why no one believes me that she says real words, because she says them any old time. Can you help me push?" We had started up a hill. I pushed on one side and Wendy pushed on the other. Pushing Jean helped me push the thoughts about my dad right out of my brain.

"Look!" I said. From the top of the hill we could see a long way. Far away to the left, circling in the sky, was the flock of white doves.

"Oh, oh, oh!" cried Wendy. "The doves! I know it's them! Jean must have heard them first." She set the brakes on the wheelchair and cupped her hands. "Call them, Bobbie Lynn. Come on."

We whistled and whistled.

Ooooo-EE-ooooo.

Jean laughed. The doves circled in the sky. They didn't come any closer, but they didn't fly away either. I stopped whistling. "Maybe they live down there some-place," I said. "We could follow them if we hurry." Wendy stopped whistling and released the brakes on Jean's chair.

"Come on!" she yelled. "Hang on to the wheelchair, like this," she said, and took the handle in one hand and then grabbed onto the side with her other hand. I did as she said and hung on tight. "Good thing Jean's strapped in," said Wendy. "Let's go."

We hurried down that hill as fast as we could without being reckless. "Jean loves to go fast," said Wendy, "but usually only my dad does it with her. Keep an eye on those doves!" They were still circling, and at the bottom of the hill we could still see them in the sky, no more than three blocks away.

"This way," I said, and we hurried the wheelchair down the street. That's when Jean began to squeal. It was a high, piercing sound, and it startled me at first.

"Keep going," said Wendy. "She's just happy." We were practically running now. A lady came out on her front porch and watched us. A man in a car slowed down and took a look. I was getting short of breath but Wendy kept pushing. "Only a block, I think," she said as she panted. When the doves were circling directly above us, we stopped. I was breathing so hard my chest hurt. "Did you see the look on that old lady's face?" Wendy started to giggle. Now Jean was making a noise like "uh, uh, uh."

"They're flying down!" yelled Wendy suddenly. "Quick, over there!" We headed down the street a little. It was lined with horse chestnut trees and curved around to the right, and suddenly it dead-ended. We stopped at a gravel driveway which led away through the trees. The late afternoon sunlight filtered through the leaves and shone on our faces. "Thataway," said Wendy.

"Are you sure?" I asked. It looked private.

"Hey!" yelled Wendy, pointing through the trees. "This is *it!*" I squinted and looked in the direction she was pointing. LITTLE SISTERS OF ST. FRANCIS.

"What is it?"

"It's the convent my mom helps clean," said Wendy. "Remember? I told you about it already. The nuns are old, and they're from some foreign country. Mom said the convent was nearby, but I didn't know it was *this* close. I wonder if she knows about the doves? Come on! Hurry! I bet the doves belong to the sisters. Ya-hoo!"

Pushing the wheelchair over gravel was not easy, but finally we got to an old brick building, two stories high with a statue in front.

"Are you sure we should be here?" I asked. "I don't want to get in trouble. Maybe this is trespassing." I'd only seen nuns on TV. They seemed scary to me, all dressed in black and white with beads on their belts. Wendy rang the doorbell.

"Don't be a worrywart," she said, but I was nervous just the same.

I didn't want to meet any nuns in black dresses. I didn't want to get yelled at, and I didn't want anyone to say, "I'm going to call your mother."

The convent door swung open. I hung on tight to the back of Jean's wheelchair.

Chapter Fourteen

The woman who opened the door wasn't dressed in black and she didn't look one bit frightening. She was dressed in brown and wore a plain brown scarf on her head. She wasn't much taller than Wendy. She was so old and hunched that she had to lean back a bit to look at us. The nun smiled, and when she did, her eyes nearly disappeared in the wrinkles around them. "Hello," she said. Her voice was quavery and on top of that she had some sort of accent. "May I help you?"

"I'm Wendy Feeney," said Wendy, "and this is Jean, and this is Bobbie Lynn. My mom is one of the Sacred Heart Circle ladies who cleans the convent for you. Mary Feeney."

"Oh yes, Mary Feeney," said the old nun. "A good soul is Mary." She nodded and looked at Wendy. "You have your mother's eyes. I am Sister Mary Clara."

"Nice to meet you, Sister," said Wendy.

"Pleased to meet you, ma'am," I said, wondering whether or not it's proper to call a nun "ma'am."

"We're looking for a flock of doves," said Wendy. I watched Sister Mary Clara's face. I'm sure I've never seen so many wrinkles. She smiled all the time Wendy was talking, and when Wendy said "doves" she nodded.

"The birds, they live here," said Sister Mary Clara, still nodding.

"I whistle at them, like this." Wendy quickly tooted through her thumbs. "They fly over my house every afternoon," she said, looking at me, "whether I whistle or not." Wendy's cheeks turned pink. She tooted once more for Sister Mary Clara.

She'd told me the doves came because she whistled. Truth was, they came anyway. Wendy was caught in a lie. For a second I was mad at her for fooling me, until I remembered all the fibs I'd been telling lately. Who was I to point the finger?

"I taught Bobbie Lynn to whistle too," said Wendy. "We did a dove duet the other day. You should hear it."

"It was very beautiful, I am sure," said Sister Mary Clara. I could tell she liked Wendy. Her eyes twinkled while she watched her talk.

"Jean here likes birds too, ma'am," I said. Sister Mary Clara looked at me and cocked her head.

"You are not from here?" she asked. I shook my head.

"I could tell by your accent," she said. "I am not from here either. Can you tell?"

"Um, no," I said. Sister Mary Clara laughed out loud.

"Oh my, such a big lie, but a polite one." Wendy and I looked at each other and laughed. "You like to bring the little girl to see the birds?"

"Yes, very, very much," said Wendy. Sister Mary Clara stepped outside and pointed around to the rear.

"See the big gate? You go there. I will meet you."
She closed the door.

"I told you not to worry," said Wendy.

"We aren't going to get in trouble for this, are we?" I
asked. "I mean, taking Jean here and everything?"

"We won't stay long," said Wendy. "I'm sure it'll
be okay."

"You said the doves came because you called them,"
I said.

"It was a lie," said Wendy. "I wanted to impress you—
that's why I said it." I didn't know what to say. If Wendy
lied to me about the doves, had she lied about other
things as well? We pushed Jean around behind the big
house. The gate was so big we couldn't see over it. We
stood there waiting, not talking. There was still no sign
of the nun.

"Will you forgive me?" whispered Wendy. "For lying?
Please?"

"'Course I will," I said, feeling swamped with embar-
rassment.

"Father Rossini always said there is no such thing as
one lie. Once you start, they just add up. Lies pile on top
of lies. That's what he said."

"He sounds like a real smart preacher," I said, wishing
I could change the subject but not knowing how.
Wendy took hold of my hand and squeezed it. Part of me
wanted to jerk away. Part of me wanted to just sit still
and let it be. I heard footsteps on the other side of the
gate. "Guess she's here," I said, and Wendy let go of my
hand. Part of me was glad. Part of me wished we were

still touching. How can one girl have so many mixed-up feelings?

Sister Mary Clara opened the gate. She had a white dove on each shoulder. She was using a cane. "Look!" she said. "They are quite tame." She shrugged and the birds fluttered up to the branches of a tree. We pushed Jean into a large brick courtyard surrounded on two sides by low buildings and on the farthest side by what looked like a little church.

"Where do the doves stay?" asked Wendy.

"Over there, that low building. Once it was a barn, then a garage for cars. Now a very big birdhouse. Listen." I could hear the gurgling and cooing as soon as she said "listen." Sister Mary Clara lowered her voice as we got closer. "They're used to me," she said. "I always speak softly to them."

When we got to the barn the sound of the doves was quite loud. Sister Mary Clara slid open a door and we looked in. There were holes in the roof that let in light. That's how the doves flew in and out. They were coming and going even as we watched them. The smell was not too bad, though Wendy held her nose at first and said, "Eeew." There were dozens, maybe hundreds, of doves. Looking at them up close I could see they weren't all white. Some of them had gray wings and heads. Others had light-brown spots.

"Jean, what do you think?" whispered Wendy. Jean sat so still I thought maybe she'd fallen asleep, until I saw her eyes. They moved from side to side, as though she were trying very hard to see what she could only hear.

"How many are there?" I asked.

"I never tried to count," said Sister Mary Clara. "What would be the use to count?"

"Tell that to Stevie," said Wendy, and we both giggled.

"Come this way, with me," said Sister Mary Clara. She closed the barn door and walked slowly across the courtyard toward a statue of a man feeding birds. "Put the little girl by Saint Francis," she said to Wendy, pointing with her cane at the statue.

"She's my sister," said Wendy. "We're twins. Can you tell?" Sister Mary Clara looked at Wendy and then at Jean.

"Yes, you look so much alike. And now I remember that Mary Feeney has twins, and you are the twins. Ah. How can I miss this? I should get glasses, yes?" She laughed when she said it so Wendy and I laughed too. "Is Jean afraid of the birds, do you think?"

"No," said Wendy. "She isn't smart enough to be afraid."

"How blessed she is," said Sister Mary Clara with a smile. "Now, you, stand very still," she said, and then she lifted up her chin as best she could and closed her eyes. "Birds, birds, birds!" she called. I held my breath and listened to the sound of wings. All of a sudden I remembered what Wendy'd said about angels, and a big old shiver ran up and down my spine.

"Birds, birds, birds!" called the nun. While she did, she fished deep into her left pocket and pulled out some grain. She sprinkled it all around us on the bricks.

The doves flapped and rustled in the barn. Then one by one, they flew up above the barn and circled us. I counted ten, and then sixteen, and then I stopped counting because they were starting to land all around and peck at the grain. I heard Wendy say "wow" under her breath. Sister Mary Clara sprinkled the grain right at our feet. The doves pecked and strutted between us. I looked at Jean. She had closed her eyes but I could tell she was listening.

"Now, look," Sister Mary Clara said. She put grain in her left hand and held it out. "Birds, come now." Two doves fluttered up and landed on her arm. She leaned hard on her cane to steady herself.

"Can I do it?" whispered Wendy. "Please?" Sister Mary Clara nodded and dug in her pockets for more grain. The doves fluttered to the ground. Wendy took some grain and gave it to me. She held out her arms and said, "Here birds. Here birds." Two doves flew up, landed on her wrists, and started pecking at the grain. "Ouch," she said. "They peck hard." I opened my hands to show the grain to the other birds.

"Birds, birds, birds," I said. Up flew a pure white dove, and landed on my wrist. "Look!" I whispered. "It's on me!" Its eyes were black and when it looked back at me, it looked sideways and tilted its head. I wanted so badly to laugh out loud. I looked at Wendy. She was grinning ear to ear.

"Now one for the little sister," said Sister Mary Clara. She coaxed one dove onto her own arm and then poured some grain into the blanket on Jean's lap. "Down here you feed," she said to the dove. "And don't peck so hard." She set the bird down gently on Jean's lap and we all waited to see what would happen. Wendy let the birds in her hands fly away and then crossed to the wheelchair. Ever so slowly, she squatted down beside Jean's knees. Jean hadn't moved an inch. Wendy took one of Jean's hands and slowly moved it toward the dove, talking softly all the time.

"There, birdie. Don't be scared. Jean can't see you with her eyes. You have to let her touch you. Don't be scared. Don't be scared. You know me. I'm your friend. I'm the one who whistles for you." Jean's hand touched the feathers. Her mouth was open and she drooled onto the front of her sweater. Wendy held her hand steady, then slowly and carefully stroked the dove's feathers with Jean's hand. The bird pecked at the grain.

"What's this, Jean?" asked Wendy. "What's this? Is it a bird?" Just then Jean threw back her head and squealed. It startled all the doves and they flew up in a white flurry of wings and tail feathers. "She definitely likes them," said Wendy. Jean squealed again, louder than before, and we all laughed.

"Could we come back again?" Wendy asked Sister Mary Clara.

"Of course, yes," said the nun. "I love visitors."

"How many people live here?" I asked.

"Only five other sisters and me," said Sister Mary Clara. "And I am the youngest." She must have noticed the surprised look on my face because she laughed. "Oh yes, I am very young. Only eighty-one. The other sisters are old. I take care of them. Now we have no children."

"What children?" asked Wendy.

But right over the top of her words I said, "Where are you from?" I hoped it wasn't rude to ask.

"From Belgium," said Sister Mary Clara. "We had an

orphanage there, destroyed by bombing during the war. An American man heard of us and gave this house and farm so here we are. We brought forty-eight children, war orphans. There were fourteen sisters then. Now only six."

"What happened to the children?" asked Wendy.

"The little ones, they were adopted by Americans. Others, they grew up. Nowadays the state takes care of the poor children, and I take care of old sisters." I thought of Mason's words. *Juvenile hall. That's how the state takes care of children now.*

"Where did the birds come from?" asked Wendy. We were through the gate and on our way around the house.

"They were always here," said Sister Mary Clara. "I feed them and they stay. And they are good company, yes." Wendy stopped pushing the wheelchair and glanced over at me.

"When the doves fly over my house some of them act like they're wounded. They fall right out of the sky and at the last minute they're okay. Why is that, Sister?"

"The falling ones, they are the tumblers. With the tumbling they distract the crows and other big birds that threaten the others."

"You mean they act hurt on purpose?" asked Wendy.

"This is true," said Sister Mary Clara. "They risk themselves for the sake of the others."

They risk themselves for the sake of others.

Those words whacked me in the head like a brick.

That's what soldiers do.

"But they get away, don't they?" I asked.

"Usually, yes," said Sister. "They are experts at surviving, even when there is much danger."

"Bobbie Lynn's dad is in Vietnam right now," Wendy said. "It's dangerous there." I stopped myself from gasping out loud. Wendy had a knack for interrupting my private thoughts, especially the ones I didn't want to talk about.

"Oh, that is very bad," said Sister Mary Clara. She put her hand on my shoulder. "What a sorrow, child, but you must not worry. I will ask his guardian angel to keep watch over him."

"See?" exclaimed Wendy. She smacked me in the arm, but not hard. "Remember what I said? It's true, isn't it, Sister? Everyone has a guardian angel."

"This is so."

"Bobbie Lynn doesn't believe it."

"I didn't say I didn't believe it." Wendy kept right on talking. I clenched my teeth together to keep from blowing up at her. I didn't want to think about Daddy, let alone hear other folks talk about him.

"Everyone has a guardian angel, me, you, your dad, everyone in the whole world, even Jean, right?" She picked up Jean's hand and held it against her cheek. "Who's this, Jean?" she asked.

Sister Mary Clara smiled so hard her eyes disappeared. She nodded and nodded. She was so thin and hunched that she looked a tad like a bird herself. "That is right. Each has an angel, especially Jean." The old nun patted Wendy's curly black hair. "And I believe I see little Jean's guardian angel. Yes. I know that angel now."

"I told you," said Wendy.

"Maybe you will do something for me?" said Sister Mary Clara. "Such a small, small favor?" I held my breath. *Please don't talk about Daddy.*

Wendy and I looked at each other and shrugged. "Sure," said Wendy.

"I wonder would you visit again, all of you, to see my old sisters? And to see the birds also. Perhaps I find a little one to send home with you. The babies are so gentle."

"I'd love a dove of my own!" said Wendy. "Jean, hear that?"

"I'd like to meet the other sisters," I said. "Do they like girls?"

"Oh, yes, yes, yes! All children," said Sister Mary Clara. "Do you have brothers and sisters?"

"I have a brother," I said.

"I have a brother and another sister," said Wendy, "but my other sister is just a baby. I think my mom would let me bring her too, but she gets into things." Sister Mary Clara was really grinning now.

"Bring them all, and your dear mother, Mary Feeney. Oh, how glad I am that God brought you to me today."

"It was the doves that brought us," said Wendy.

"Yes, the doves," said Sister Mary Clara, nodding all the while she spoke. "But they work for Him, you know." She pointed up to the sky and we all laughed.

"I'd like to come back again, ma'am," I said. "I'd like it very much." I felt my voice catch in my throat. What was it about this place, about this old woman who never stopped smiling? It's hard to put into words how it all made me feel. Maybe safe is a good word for it. A smile crept up my cheeks. I wanted to come back in a big way.

"Do you think Jean could have her own dove?" asked Wendy. "I mean if I promise to take care of it for her?"

"I am sure," said Sister Mary Clara.

All of a sudden I had the powerful urge to open up my mouth and tell Wendy and Sister Mary Clara that Daddy was missing in action. It was like the secret was swelling inside me, pushing to get out. One minute I was mad at Wendy for talking about Daddy being in Vietnam. The next minute I was all happy thinking about coming back to visit Sister Mary Clara.

If I told about Daddy, there would be questions. Mason was right. If I said a word, and they found out about Mama and the gun and all, we would end up in the juvenile hall. And Mama? What would they do to her? How could one girl have so many terrible big feelings? I had to clamp my lips together to keep from telling more.

I bit the inside of my cheek. There was something about Sister Mary Clara that made me want to tell it all. Maybe it was because she knew about war or about kids. Maybe it was because she was friendly and nice and old, like a granny.

Sister Mary Clara waved at us. "Come again," she said.

"We will," said Wendy

I will, I said inside my head, and then I helped wheel Jean down the gravel drive.

Chapter Fifteen

"We'd better hurry," said Wendy. "My mom will worry if we're gone too long." She picked up her pace as we headed up the hill. "Wasn't that exciting?"

"That sister was mighty nice," I said, helping to push Jean. "I think she liked us." *What would she have done if I'd told her about Daddy being missing?*

"Of course she liked us," said Wendy. "Nuns have to like everyone. It's their job. Most of them are pretty good at it, except the crabby ones."

"I loved the doves," I said. *A nun who'd been in World War II would know about soldiers being missing in action.* "Did their feet feel warm to you?"

"Warm and pokey," said Wendy. "I had to bite my tongue so I wouldn't laugh and scare them away."

"Same here," I said. I thought about what Sister Mary Clara had said about their orphanage being destroyed by bombs. There were bombs in Vietnam. I hadn't thought about bombs ruining good places like orphanages, or hurting good people like nuns and children. Were there nuns in Vietnam? And orphanages? Why was it that a war far away didn't seem too very real? Who was the enemy anyhow? What kind of person would shoot down a plane my daddy was flying in? The enemy, that's who. Had someone thought Sister Mary Clara and her orphans were bad? Had they thought she was the enemy? Only bad people would shoot and hurt other people. No, that wasn't right. Daddy would shoot too. And he wasn't a bad person. And now he was missing, and maybe that meant dead. I swallowed down the confused feelings that had crept up and begun to choke me. Just a few minutes back I'd felt so safe I'd almost told everything. Now here I was all worked up, and those words wanted to fall right out of my mouth. Why was it so hard to push them down?

Keep the secret, you big fool, I scolded myself. We were at the top of the hill and heading down the other side toward our own neighborhood. "Time to go fast again, Jean," said Wendy. "She sure was quiet today."

"Except for when she squealed at the birds," I said. *Could I tell a small part of the secret?*

"I liked the way Sister Mary Clara called the doves," said Wendy. "Next time they fly over I'm going to try it. Birds! Birds! Birds!" Jean moaned. "Uh-oh. Are we going too fast?" Wendy asked Jean.

"Wah," said Jean.

"What does that mean?" I asked. *Maybe just the missing in action part?*

"Beats me," said Wendy.

"You told me earlier that 'wah' meant 'hi.'" Wendy leaned in my direction and whispered.

"Sometimes I act like I'm sure when I'm not. It's not the same as lying."

I didn't have anything to say to this. Was that true? Was feeling or thinking one way and acting another the same as a lie? I hoped not. If so I'd told an awful lot of lies in my life without ever opening my mouth. There were always secrets to keep at our house, about Mama and her problems. I was doing it just then, wanting to tell about Daddy, and keeping my mouth shut. Why did keeping secrets feel so much like lying?

"Bub," said Jean.

"Hey!" said Wendy. "She said 'birds.' Say it again, Jean. Come on. Birds, birds, birds."

"Do you really think she understands?" I asked.

"I do," said Wendy. "No one else does, but I DO. Birds, birds, birds, Jean."

"Bub," said Jean. "Bub, bub, bub, bub, bub."

"Hey!" said Wendy. "Listen! Hear that?"

"Bub, bub, bub, bub, bub, bub."

"She's saying it! She's calling the birds!" I didn't know if Jean was really talking, but she sure was making a racket. Wendy joined in as we pushed.

"Bub, bub, bub, bub," they said. Pretty soon I wanted to giggle.

"You can say it too," said Wendy. "Bub, bub, bub." We both laughed out loud. Jean was still saying "bub."

"Bub," I said. "There, I said it." Wendy laughed so hard she doubled over and we had to stop the wheelchair.

"You have to say it a whole bunch of times," she said. Jean was still chanting. I felt silly but now Wendy was shouting. "BUB, BUB, BUB!" Jean started to squeal and that's when I couldn't hold it anymore.

"Bub, bub, BUB!" I hollered. "Okay, I said it."

"Race you home," said Wendy, and she started pushing the wheelchair so fast I had to run to keep up. We ran practically all the way to Wendy's house. Jean squealed sometimes and said "bub" sometimes, and everyone who saw us stared. Wendy's hair was a mess when she got home, and her cheeks were as red as cherry Popsicles. I was so out of breath that I had a fit of coughing.

"I'd best go now," I said when I could finally talk. "Thanks for asking me along."

"I'm glad you came," said Wendy, brushing a mess of curls out of her face. "And I am really, really, really glad we saw the doves and met Sister Mary Clara! I can't wait to visit her again. I can't wait to tell my mom."

I was going to be polite and just say "good-bye" and "see you tomorrow at school" and "I hope Jean had a good time too," but that's not what came out. I don't know why I said it. The words were out before I could stop them.

"Do you know what MIA means?" I asked, and before Wendy could answer I heard the words tumble out of my mouth like they belonged to someone else. "My daddy is MIA and that's missing in action, if you didn't know it already." Wendy's mouth dropped open.

"When?" she asked.

"'While back," I said, now feeling the red heat on my face that had nothing to do with running. I don't know what I expected. No, I didn't expect anything, least of all that I'd go and tell it to Wendy. "I figured if y'all are praying on account of him being in Vietnam, well, you ought to know the full truth of it." I couldn't look up. I looked at the place where the wheels of Jean's chair met the sidewalk. There was a bit of grass growing between a crack in the cement. How was it grass always could find the smallest bit of dirt to grow in? Just then I coughed some more.

"Are you getting a cold?" asked Wendy.

"No," I said, and coughed two more times.

"How come you never said anything before?" asked Wendy. I shrugged. "Do you think they'll find him?" I shrugged again. Now the hated tears were coming. I blinked and set my jaw, grinding my teeth together so hard it hurt all the way to my eyeballs. I got the tiniest piece of my inside lower lip between my teeth and bit again. *Don't cry, don't cry, don't cry.* It worked.

Wendy didn't know what else to say. I could tell. And it was a good thing too, because she didn't ask a single question after that.

"See you at school then," I said. "Bye, Jean." Jean swung her head in my direction.

"Bub," she said.

"No, Jean, Bobbie Lynn," said Wendy quietly.

"Please tell your mother thanks for dinner," I said. "It was real good."

"Okay, I will," said Wendy. Telling her had made her upset. Why had I been so stupid? Now she felt sorry for me. Now she didn't know what to say. The air between us felt thick as Jell-O pudding. Wendy seemed like a stranger now, not a friend who'd just done a whole lot of laughing on a nice long walk. That's what happens when a blabbermouth tells a secret that someone else doesn't want to hear. Mason would kill me if he ever found out.

"Gotta go," I said.

"All right," said Wendy. I looked up. She was frowning at me. It wasn't a mad frown, though.

"Bye," I said again.

"Bye, Bobbie Lynn," said Wendy. "You know I'll say a bunch of prayers." I said that would be fine, thank you, and then I turned and started down the block toward home.

I wished I could kick myself in the behind for telling. Why'd I done it? Telling Wendy had been like spraying poison all over her. She didn't need to know about Daddy. Now she was sad and I felt worse than before. She'd treat me strange from now on. That's what people do when they know bad secrets about you. Stupid me. Stupid, stupid, stupid.

I thought about the doves and Sister Mary Clara and how happy I'd felt for a few minutes. I thought about yelling "bub" with Jean. If you think about it too much, feeling happy feels awful strange when it's not the way you're used to feeling. When it's over you think, why did I act so happy when so many things are wrong?

Would a few extra prayers make a difference? Deep down I didn't think so. God hadn't been paying attention to our family for a long, long time.

When a balloon is blown up too tight it's easy to pop, but if you let some of the air out, well then, you can play with it for days if you're careful. Telling Wendy about Daddy was like letting some air out of the balloon in my heart and it felt good. That's the best way I can think to say it.

Mason wouldn't find out. Why should he? I'd have to make sure Wendy didn't tell a soul about Daddy being missing. For sure Mrs. Saunders couldn't find out. I'd call Wendy later and tell her not to tell. I'd explain how Mama was sensitive about such things, how she was delicate and fretful. That wouldn't be a lie at all. It would be the truth.

I got home expecting Mason to be there. He was nowhere in sight. Where was he? He'd said he'd come home right after school. I'd give that boy a piece of my mind when I found him. When I peeked in on Mama, I forgot all about Mason. Soon as I opened the door the smell almost knocked me flat.

"Mama?" I asked. "What's wrong?" I held my breath and crept into the dark room. I fought the urge to retch. When I got to Mama's bedside I saw what had happened. Mama had thrown up in bed and no one had cleaned it up. I was already mad at Mason for not being home. Now my anger boiled inside me like a teakettle on the stove. Where was he? Mama seemed peaceful enough now. It was probably just a touch of the flu. Had she called for help? Where was Mason, anyway?

I was mad at myself too, not just Mason. How could I have thought Mama was doing better? And then, to be truthful, there was a tiny bit of mad I felt at Mama too. She was a grownup. How could she expect a couple of kids like me and Mason to take care of her every minute of the day? And why hadn't she gotten up to be sick? So far she'd been able to get up to go to the bathroom. She'd been able to smoke and rock for hours in her chair. Then I felt furious at myself for even thinking these things, and got busy cleaning things up. I was supposed to feel sorry for Mama, but the fact is, the sorry was mixed with too many other things to be pure sorry.

Cleaning up the mess was a real chore. Mama woke up when I started to pull the blankets off her, but she only stared off into space and didn't say a word. I had to change the sheets like I'd seen a nurse do on *General Hospital*, with Mama in the bed.

Luckily, Mama had missed her nightgown when she threw up, but then I thought about how she'd had that same nightgown on for days, how she hadn't had a bath or anything, and I realized she wasn't clean at all and she wasn't about to help herself.

"Mama?" I said right next to her head. She opened her eyes and looked at me but she didn't know it was me. I could tell. "Do you want to put on a new nightgown?" I asked. She closed her eyes. All of a sudden, my legs felt too tired to hold me up. I knelt at the bedside and put my face on the clean sheets I'd just put on the mattress. They felt cool and smelled good, like laundry soap.

"Where have you gone, Mama?" I whispered. Didn't she know she was breaking my heart? I stroked her cheek and traced the shape of her eyebrow with my finger. She always plucked her eyebrows so thin. Her face was hot and dry. "Please come back."

She didn't mean to shoot at you, God. It was a mistake.

I lay with my face beside her like that for a while, I don't know how long, until she stirred some.

"Thirsty," she said, and I jumped up to get her a drink. Jumping up like that made my head spin. I had to go out of the room and down the hall to the bathroom. What would happen if Mama got so bad she couldn't get up to go to the bathroom anymore? Could she get that bad?

How much longer could we all hold out?

I brought her water and helped her sit up to drink it. "You threw up," I said. "Are you all right now?" She nodded. "Where's Mason?" I asked. She closed her eyes again and lay back without a word. If anyone found out, if they put us in the juvenile hall, who would take proper care of Mama? I blinked back the tears thinking about it.

Nobody loves you like we do, Mama.

There was something I needed to do.

I went downstairs and called Wendy's house. There on the chalkboard was Aunt Jeri Lee's number. I stared at it and wondered what Austin was like. I wondered if Aunt Jeri Lee still had blonde hair. Beauticians change their hair all the time. The phone rang at the Feeneys'. I wondered if Aunt Jeri Lee would like my pixie haircut. The phone rang again. Would she really call back in a month like she'd said? Wendy's phone rang once more before Stevie answered. "Feeney residence," he said.

"Hi, Stevie," I said. "May I speak to Wendy, please?" He didn't answer, but I heard him put the phone down hard and then I heard footsteps. Wendy was on the phone in seconds.

"Hi," she said. "Stevie said it was you."

"Just wanted to ask you a favor," I said.

"Okay," said Wendy.

"Well," I hesitated. I had to say it just right so she didn't ask a lot of questions. I didn't want to have to lie too much. "Remember I told you that thing that happened to my dad?"

"You mean that he's missing?" I didn't like hearing the words from someone else, not even over the phone. I took a deep breath.

"That's right," I said. "See, my mama is particular about privacy. She doesn't want a lot of folks to know about Daddy. She said it would only make them feel sorry for us, you know, like we're pathetic." It was partly true and partly untrue. Would Wendy know I wasn't telling the whole truth?

"You mean don't talk about it?" asked Wendy.

"If you don't mind," I said. "Especially at school, you know, Mrs. Saunders, the other kids."

"I told my mom and dad," said Wendy. "I didn't know it was private."

Too late! I felt a touch of panic but I kept my voice calm.

"Oh, they can know, but tell them what I said about Mama being touchy."

"I will," said Wendy. "And I told one other person." I swallowed down my fear but didn't say a word. "I told Sister Mary Clara, you know, at the convent. Mom said we could all go visit her and the other sisters on Sunday so I called to tell her, and that's when I told her about your dad, since we'd been talking about it. Want to come with us when we go?"

"Sure," I said.

"You didn't tell me it was a secret."

If I could have kicked myself just then I would have done it.

"Not a secret, just private."

"Are you mad?" asked Wendy.

"No," I said. How could I be mad? It was my own stupid fault. I'd known better than to tell.

"Can I ask you something?" said Wendy.

"I suppose," I said, dreading what might come next.

"How come you didn't tell me sooner?" asked Wendy. "If it was me I would have told you the very day."

"I couldn't," I said simply, and that was the truth too, because Mason had made me swear not to. Thinking of Mason made that mad feeling come back. I looked at the clock on the living-room wall. It was quarter past six and he wasn't home yet. "I have to go," I said.

"Okay," said Wendy. "I'm not mad about your not telling me," she added. "I'm sad about it. That's all. I'm glad you told me. And I swear I won't tell another soul, cross my heart and hope to die, stick a needle in my eye."

"All right," I said. I heard Wendy's mom in the background.

"My mom is asking if your mom needs anything."

"Oh," I said, feeling my heartbeat pick up, "no, she doesn't need a thing. She'd rather not talk about it, you know? She keeps to herself when she's upset."

"Okay, I'll tell her that," said Wendy. She sounded so different than usual, so dull and sad, not bright and sassy and ready to pick a fight with anyone who got in her way. "Mom thought it was cool about the doves and us meeting Sister Mary Clara."

I thought I heard Mama just then. I wasn't sure but I didn't want her to start up with Wendy on the phone.

"I have to get off the phone," I said, trying to sound cheerful and hoping desperately that Wendy had not heard anything. "I have to clean my room." It was getting easy to lie. I hadn't wanted to fib. It just came out. Was lying becoming automatic? Was that what Wendy's Father Rossini had meant when he said lies pile on top of lies?

"See you at school tomorrow," said Wendy. "And don't forget about Sunday. Sister Mary Clara said we could look for babies in the barn."

"That'd suit me fine," I said. "Bye now," I said, and before Wendy could say good-bye too, I'd hung up the phone with a bang.

I ran up and checked on Mama. Running up the stairs gave me another fit of coughing. "Are you okay?" I asked as soon as I could get my breath. "You need something to eat or drink?" I asked. She didn't say. She just stared right past me and shook her head. Maybe she hadn't called me. Maybe I was hearing things. I was too tired to puzzle over it. I went downstairs and flipped on the TV set.

I don't like the news usually, but that's what I turned to first. I was just about to look for something good when Walter Cronkite said, "Fifty thousand people have gathered in Washington, D.C., today to protest continued U.S. involvement in Vietnam." The camera showed crowds and crowds of people. Some were holding up big signs. Others were singing. A lot of the people looked like hippies but some of them looked like regular enough folks. There were white people and Negro people, all together. Some people had brought babies and little kids. There were police all over too. I never saw so many people in one place. Walter Cronkite started to talk but I didn't hear what he said because all I could hear was this big group yelling over and over, "DOWN WITH WAR! DOWN WITH WAR! DOWN WITH WAR!"

I watched more of that news show, until they started to show fighting in Vietnam and then I turned it off. Who was right? The people who wanted to stop the war or the people like my daddy who wanted to stop communism? It had seemed so clear whenever Daddy had talked about it before. Now I wasn't sure. Where was Mason?

It was way past suppertime but I didn't feel hungry. I made some toast for Mama and took it up, but she didn't want to eat and I didn't try to make her. I just let her be. The house felt cold to me. Should I turn on the heat? We hadn't used it yet, and I wasn't sure how to do it.

I got a sweater our of my dresser drawer, and when that wasn't enough, I got a sweatshirt too. I was still cold. A couple of times my teeth chattered, just like a cartoon character. I coughed now and then and it hurt to cough.

I watched show after show and tried not to think about the news. Where was Mason? What would I do if he was missing? I couldn't think about it long, because it sent a panicky feeling up my spine that was so strong it made my ears buzz. My head was hurting too. Too much TV, I thought. Daddy always said too much would rot my brain.

At nine o'clock Mama called down and asked for a glass of water. I took it to her and helped her drink.

Where could Mason be? I didn't want to worry about him. Why couldn't I get that boy out of my head?

By now I was so cold I was shivering all the time. I ran the water in the bath. A hot bath would warm me up. I stripped and lowered myself into the hot, steaming water. It gave me goose bumps all over, but it didn't warm me. Wherever my wet skin was exposed to the air, I felt cold. Even with my whole self underwater, I shivered. I tried going all the way under, even my head. When I wiped the water out of my eyes I noticed the faint outline of Wendy's phone number on my hand. I should have washed it off but I didn't have the will.

I got out, dried off, and dressed for bed. I looked at the clock and saw it was quarter past ten. I got two extra blankets out of my closet and piled them on the bed. I crawled in between the sheets and lay there freezing, wishing I could get warm, wishing my head would stop hurting, wishing Mason would come home. I'd give him what for the minute I laid eyes on him. Where was that boy?

What would I do without him?

Chapter Sixteen

I dreamed I was in a tunnel and cars were speeding past me on either side. The drivers couldn't see me because it was dark, so I had to dodge the cars as fast as they came. I ran and dodged until I was so out of breath my chest hurt.

I am out of breath, like something is pressing on me, flattening me. . . . Car tires are rolling on me and I can't get away and I can't even get a breath to holler for help. . . .

And that's when the sound of the back door woke me up. I rubbed my eyes. My heart started to race, until I figured it must be Mason. I rolled over to get out of bed and felt a tightness in my chest, a dull pain like the out-of-breath feeling in my nightmare. Rolling over made my head pound. I couldn't quite catch my breath. How could a dream be so real? I coughed but it didn't help. I heard footsteps coming upstairs. It had to be Mason.

Please let it be Mason.

When my bedroom door opened I was sitting on the edge of the bed. I was so cold I'd pulled the covers around me like a cape. My eyes were used to the dark, but I couldn't see who it was.

"Mason?" I whispered, and then I coughed. My chest hurt like crazy. A shadowy figure stepped into my room. Before I could see his face, I knew it was Mason. I could smell his Ivory soap and sweat.

"Hi," he said. He closed the door and switched on my light. I squinted and hid my face. I tried to take a deep breath.

"Ouch," I said. Why did breathing hurt so much?

"How come you're all wrapped up like that?" asked Mason.

"I'm freezing," I said. "And where have you been, anyhow?" Mason looked down and kicked at the edge of the red and green braided rug.

"Had some stuff to do," he said. "Mama was asleep, so I didn't think it would matter if I left."

"She was sick, you idiot!" I said, trying to keep my voice down. "She puked all over her bed. I had to clean it up. You said you'd be home right after school." On the inside I was so mad I could spit, but I didn't have the spunk to give him *what* for. I felt like there was a man with a hammer in my head. I lay down on my side, still wrapped like a mummy in the blankets. "Go away," I said, and then I coughed some more. "I don't want to see your ugly face." I closed my eyes and lay there, wishing I could get a deep breath, wishing Mama were well enough to bring some aspirin and fuss over me. Tears tried to squeeze out from my eyes so I closed them even tighter. Last thing I was going to do was ask that no-good brother of mine for aspirin or let him see me cry.

"Don't you want to know where I was?" he asked. I opened one eye and glanced at my clock. It was eleven-thirty-five. "What's wrong with you, anyhow? You look like you saw a ghost."

"My head hurts," I said. "If Mama was well she'd threaten to beat the tar out of you for being out so late."

Mason rolled his eyes. He knew as well as I that Mama never hit.

"I went to see Mama's boss." He kicked at the rug some more. "Right after school."

"Oh."

"Mama's fired."

All the mad went out of me just like if you stepped on a raw egg on the sidewalk and smashed it flat. I lay in my bed without moving. Outside a car drove by. I could hear Mason breathing. I could hear my own heart inside my chest and the quick rhythm of the heartbeat on my eardrums. "Did you ask if she could have some more days?"

"'Course I did, stupid. He said even if she were in the hospital it wouldn't matter. He's got a store to run. She was only part-time. That means she doesn't have the same kind of rights. That's what he said."

No job, no money. We were in big, big trouble now. Somewhere inside me, I knew I should feel worried but I was too tired.

"I asked Mama's boss if I could have a job, bagging groceries, carrying things, anything. But he said no. I checked a bunch of other places, the drug store, the Arctic Circle Drive-In, Hansen's Hardware, the Dairy Queen. No one believed I was sixteen." Mason nibbled at a hangnail on his thumb. He looked so small and grubby that even I could barely believe he was thirteen.

"I went and hocked my bike," said Mason. I gasped when he said it because I was so surprised, and it made me start coughing. I coughed a dozen or so times. I'd never had a cough that hurt so bad. Finally I was able to talk.

"I can't believe you did it," I said, but I surely did believe it. Maybe Mason wasn't so no-good after all.

"I got thirty-eight dollars. Took the bike downtown to a pawn shop. They liked it real well, said it was in good shape. Should be, being practically brand new," said Mason, and then he straightened up his shoulders and kept talking. "I walked home. That took a couple hours. Didn't want to spend any money on the bus. I stopped by that all-night grocery. Picked up some stuff."

I wanted to tell him how worried I'd been but I felt so awful I could hardly move. Mama's voice broke the silence. "Jimmy?" she called. Mason and I exchanged looks. I saw Mason suck in the side of one cheek and bite it. "Jimmy?" called Mama. I closed my eyes again and wished my head would stop pounding.

"I'll check on her," said Mason. He sounded dog tired himself. I was going to tell him to see if Mama needed a drink of water, but when I tried to talk all that came out was coughing. "When did you get a cold?" asked Mason.

"Today," I managed to croak.

"That's all we need around here," muttered Mason on his way out. "Another sick person." He switched off the light and shut the door behind him and I was left in the dark to shiver and cough until I drifted back to sleep, back to the bad dreams and all the smothering feelings that filled up my aching head.

Chapter Seventeen

I'm at the edge of an ocean. The water is coming at me, surging in and out like the surf, but it isn't water, it's flaming lava, and I have to dodge sideways and keep an eye on it while I try to run away, and my lungs are so full of smoke from the burning lava waves that I can hardly breathe. I'm so hot I want to take all my clothes off. I'm in a furnace, running, breathing the hot, smothering smoke.

Smoke.

Flaming lava smoke.

Run, Bobbie Lynn Brewer. Run. Run for your life.

I awoke with a jerk and looked at the clock. I'd only slept half an hour. How could so much happen in a dream in so short a time? I coughed and coughed. I held my chest tight with my arms, trying to hold the pain so it wouldn't be so bad. I was so hot that I was sweating. My pajama top stuck to me. I threw off the covers and fanned myself. The burning dream smell was still in my nose.

But it wasn't any dream. I smelled smoke all right. Cigarette smoke. Then I heard Mama call my name.

"Bobbie Lynn?"

I crawled out of bed. How could breathing and moving hurt so much? I put on my bathrobe, turned on the light, and dragged myself down to Mama's room. Her door was open and the cigarette smoke clung to the ceiling like a cloud. The lights were out in her room but I could see the glowing end of her cigarette. The smell made me cough. The pain in my head hammered without letting up. Why couldn't she let me sleep?

"What do you need, Mama?" I asked. The smoke made me cough.

I crossed to her bed and switched on her little bedside lamp. She flinched from the light. Her skin was almost gray and so were her lips. I coughed again, so hard it made my ears ring, but Mama didn't seem to notice.

"I had a real bad dream," she said.

"Me too," I said. I brushed a messy strand of hair out of Mama's face. How could a grown-up person look so much like a little child? "But bad dreams disappear like when you pop a soap bubble, soon as you wake up. You always told me that, when I was small."

"Did I?" she said.

"Yeah, you did," I said. "Then you'd make me tell you the dream and you'd laugh at all the scary parts so I could see how silly it all was. 'Member?"

And you took care of me when I was sick, instead of the other way around. Remember?

I coughed again. I wanted to tell Mama how much my head hurt, but what use would it be? Mama's room felt like an oven. How could she sleep at all?

"I dreamed Daddy went off to war," said Mama. She stared across the room. Her tears spilled out onto her cheeks and trickled down. She took a drag on her cigarette. "I knew a boy who went to war once," she whispered. "But that time it wasn't a dream."

My knees felt weak. I wanted to sit down so bad. What could I say? Was I supposed to tell her it wasn't a dream? Or was I supposed to lie, tell her Daddy would be home tomorrow? I crossed the room and sat in the rocking chair. Mama just smoked. My ears rang and my head spun and Mama seemed to get real small, real far away.

"It's no dream," I whispered. "Not any of it." I watched as the ash at the end of Mama's cigarette got longer and longer. "Don't let the ash drop, Mama!" I said, but it was too late. Just then the telephone rang downstairs.

I jumped up. It hurt something silly to move that fast. I coughed and coughed, so hard I thought I might not be able to stop or get my breath. I crossed the room to Mama's bed and swept the ashes off the blankets. Too late. The ash had burned a black hole. The phone rang again. I was about to yell for Mason to go answer it when I noticed the other black holes, holes Mama had burned in her own blankets. I counted seven.

The phone rang again, and then it was quiet. Who'd call in the middle of the night anyway? I put it out of my mind and lifted up Mama's blankets. Underneath there were cigarette burns on the sheets too, and some of the burns were an inch across, like the ash had smoldered there for a long time before going out. These were fresh sheets. All these burns were from one day, no, not even a whole day.

I went into the bathroom and dug through the hamper. I looked over the old sheets, the dirty ones I'd taken off her bed that afternoon, and there were burns on them too. How could I have missed it before?

Something inside snapped. I didn't give a thought to what I should do next. I went back to Mama's room and gathered up all the cigarettes. Mama had just lit up a fresh one. I took it out from between her fingers and smashed it out in the ashtray and broke it up so she couldn't relight it.

"Why'd you do that?" she asked. She sounded like a bewildered little girl.

"No more cigarettes," I said. I felt under her pillow. I found her lighter there. My hands trembled and I felt lightheaded. My eyeballs were hurting now, like someone was trying to poke them out. I coughed hard.

"Bobbie Lynn?" Mama struggled to prop herself up on one elbow. "You have no right to be so mean to me!" I saw new tears well up in her tired, hollow eyes. "No one cares about me," she said, and then she began to cry real loud. I heard Mason's door open.

"It's for your own good, Mama," I said, choking down the sobs that wanted to stop up my throat. "And of course we care for you. Who's been taking care of you for all these days?" I couldn't believe how sassy I sounded. I didn't care. "You're going to burn the house down, Mama. Do you want that?" She stared at me with the blankest look I'd ever seen. "Daddy said you can't smoke in bed. I'm just doing what he says, for your sake."

"Where is he?" asked Mama. "I'll ask him myself. He'll let me do anything I want." I searched Mama's drawer without answering her and found two more packs of cigarettes. I was shaking so hard I could hardly keep my hands steady. "You go to sleep," I said, trying to sound soothing, trying to sound like Mama'd sounded to me when I was the child and she was the grown-up mother.

"I can't!" cried Mama. "You know I can't sleep when Jimmy's gone." Mason stepped into the room.

"What's wrong?" he said, rubbing his eyes. "Who called?"

"Jimmy?" said Mama. "Is that you?"

I pushed past Mason without explaining. There was a motor inside me that kept me going even though I didn't have the power to go. I hurried down the hallway and into the bathroom. I dumped all the cigarettes down the toilet and flushed. Then I went downstairs.

I felt clumsy and trembly. What did I want? What should I do? I couldn't breathe. I coughed. I gagged and coughed again. Tears made everything too blurry to see. I picked up the telephone.

"What's got into you?" yelled Mason from upstairs. His voice startled me and I dropped the phone. I picked it up and started to dial O for Operator, but then I coughed and couldn't stop and couldn't get my breath. Aunt Jeri Lee's number was still on the chalkboard.

I could call Aunt Jeri Lee.

I coughed into my hand and saw phlegm with what looked like streaks of blood. I stared at my hand and sank to the floor, wiping my hand clean on the carpet, and there it was, faint but still readable, BR for the street Sears is on, 4 for all the Feeney kids, 1225 for Christmas.

I dialed Wendy's number. Her mom answered the phone.

"Hello?" said Mrs. Feeney. She sounded awful sleepy.

"This is Bobbie Lynn," I said. "Wendy's friend." A sob broke loose. I couldn't talk.

"Bobbie Lynn?" said Mrs. Feeney. Now she was wide awake. "What's wrong? What's happened?" I caught my breath and said the hardest words of my life.

"I need help."

I started to cough again. I coughed until I thought my chest would split open from the terrible pain, and then my ears started to buzz and everything turned black. The last thing I remember was falling in the darkness until something hard stopped my fall and then everything was still and quiet as a graveyard.

Chapter Eighteen

I heard unfamiliar voices. I opened my eyes and stared up at the ceiling. A face came into view. It was a stranger's face, a red-faced man with a crew cut. Another face looked at me. This one I'd seen. It was a worried face. I coughed. The pain ripped through my chest. Now I remembered. It was Mrs. Feeney, Wendy's mom. I'd called her and here she was, just like that. She put her hand on my cheek and I knew she was real.

"You fainted, Bobbie Lynn. You're very, very sick." I moved my head to one side and saw ambulance people coming down the stairs with a stretcher. I tried to sit up but Mrs. Feeney held me down. "No, dear. Lie still." The stretcher passed us. I could see Mama, wrapped almost as tight as a mummy. She was small and pale and her body hardly made a bump on that stretcher.

"They're taking your mother to the hospital," said Mrs. Feeney. "Your brother told us everything. I wish we'd known, honey." Suddenly I couldn't resist anymore. I swallowed and let my tears come. I was too tired to fight them. They dripped down the sides of my face. Pain, relief, fear, they all jostled one another in a race to get out of my heart in the form of those tears. Tears that wouldn't stop, tears that splashed around as I shivered.

"Mason?" I managed to squeak out, afraid I'd start coughing but needing desperately to know where my big brother was. I didn't care if he was furious with me for calling Mrs. Feeney. I didn't even care if he yelled at me.

"He's fine," said Mrs. Feeney. Just then she turned and looked toward the front door.

"Wendy called the smelter," said a soft, deep voice. I blinked enough tears away to see. "They let me off an hour early." It was Mr. Feeney, tall, thin, quiet as he'd been when I'd met him. It seemed like a strange dream to me but I knew it was real because when I coughed it hurt and in between coughing I shivered with cold. Mrs. Feeney saw me shivering and took an afghan off the couch. She put it over me but it didn't help. The ambulance people came back with the stretcher. A man dressed like a policeman came in and started talking to Mrs. Feeney. Why would a policeman be at our house? I didn't think about it long.

"Your turn, baby doll," said a husky man in a blue overall. I started to protest but Mrs. Feeney put her hand on my face again.

"You've got a terrible fever," she said. "And that cough." She shook her head. "You need to go to the hospital too."

"No," I said weakly.

"Yeah, you go on now, Bobbie Lynn," said Mason. I hadn't heard him come up behind me. He squatted by my head. I waited for the scolding but it didn't come.

"How long has she been sick?" asked the ambulance

man. He lowered the stretcher and started to move me. Mr. Feeney helped.

"Just today, sir," said Mason. "It came on hard and sudden. That right?" I nodded. The ambulance man wrapped me in a blanket. I felt a little warmer. How could having a fever make me feel so cold? People were talking, people were moving around, moving me. I felt like a rag doll. If they'd wanted to tie me in knots I couldn't have resisted.

"How long has your mother been feeling bad, son?" asked the ambulance man. I looked at my brother. He seemed so small and thin and tired. His shoulder slumped and his face was smudged with dirt. There were streaks in the dirt where tears had slipped down his cheeks. Mason played with the edge of his pajama sleeve.

"Little over a week," said Mason and his eyes met mine. *Let's not lie anymore,* I wanted to say, but I was too weak. Mason sniffed and wiped his nose. "No, that's not true," he said. "Fact is, she's been sick a long time."

They wheeled me out to the street. I saw neighbors lined up and down the block to watch. The only one I recognized was Mr. Steward. We hadn't lived there long enough to know the other folks around us. I should have felt embarrassed at all the fuss, but the fact is, I didn't care. The ambulance said ST. JOSEPH'S HOSPITAL in white letters on the side. I think it was blue or maybe gray. They put me into the ambulance right smack next to Mama. Just as they were closing up the back doors a phone rang someplace far away. I turned my head so I could see Mama's chest go up and down with each breath.

"Mama?" I said. Was she asleep? She stirred and turned her head in my direction. Her eyes were open and I could see she was scared. I tried to smile. "Everything's gonna be okay," I said.

"Where are they taking me?" Her voice was so small I could barely hear it.

"To see the doctor," I said. I coughed. "I'll go with you, okay?" Mama closed her eyes and didn't say anything, but I thought I saw her nod just a little.

I had a bad coughing spell, so bad I turned and threw up over the side of the stretcher in the ambulance, and then I couldn't get my breath, and next thing I knew, they stuck a needle in me, put an oxygen mask on my face, and then I was at the hospital being wheeled here and there, up the elevator, down long hallways, into the x-ray place. I remember being cold and worrying about Mama. And I remember that I was too tired to be nervous or scared even when they stuck a needle in the back of my hand and hooked me to a bottle of clear liquid. I remember two nurses helping roll me into a bed after that. I grabbed one of them by the wrist.

"My mama?" I said.

"They'll take good care of her, honey," said the nurse.

"My brother?" The nurse stopped and thought a second and looked at the other nurse.

"I don't know about your brother," she said. The other nurse shook her head and shrugged. "I'm sure he's fine.

You try to sleep now." They put extra blankets on the bed and tucked me in.

If I slept, I don't remember it. I thought about that policeman in our house and then it made sense. There was only one place Mason could be right now. Juvenile hall, with all the criminal boys. The policeman had come to take us away. When I was out of the hospital, I'd have to go there too. Had Wendy's mom called the police? I stared at the hospital-room ceiling, just like Mason would be staring at the jail ceiling across town.

When the sun peeked through the drapes I saw there was a crucifix just above the door, like Wendy's. I looked at it for a long time, then I did something I'd never done. "God," I whispered. "Please, Sir, send one of those angels to take care of Mason at juvenile hall." I remembered Wendy's words about everyone having a guardian angel, everyone in the whole world. "And please send one to take care of Mama," I bit my lower lip and felt the familiar tears fill up my eyes, "and one to take care of Daddy in Vietnam."

A little while later I felt warm enough to close my eyes. I guess I dozed some, because when I opened them again there was a nun all dressed in white sitting in the chair beside my bed. I hadn't heard her come in. She had the prettiest, perkiest smile on her face and the kind of skin Mama calls peaches and cream. Usually I don't like strangers touching me, but when she reached over and took my hand I didn't mind.

"Good morning, dear," said the nun. "You've had a hard week, haven't you?" I nodded. Were there nuns all over this town? I figured she must be a nurse. I looked for her name tag but didn't see one. "You can call me Sister Therese," said the nun. She laid her hand on my forehead for a minute and closed her eyes. "There," she said after a minute. She had such a big smile. "That's better."

Sister Therese was real young and she had green eyes that were sparkly bright with yellow flecks. Her eyebrows were so blonde they looked golden. I wondered what color her hair was under that tight white headdress she wore. She felt my pulse and smiled the whole time. "Bathroom or bedpan?" she asked, and suddenly I realized how much I needed to go.

"Bathroom, please," I said. Sister Therese helped me out of bed. I was still hooked to that bottle but it was on a stand with wheels so I rolled it along to the little bathroom. The floor was cold and so was the toilet seat. When I finished I went out and Sister Therese was waiting for me. She tucked me into bed.

"Warm now?" she asked. I nodded. She showed me the little push-button by my bed and said to call if I needed anything at all. I said I would.

It's hard to describe exactly how I felt just then. I'm kind of old to be fussed over, but it felt so good to have that nun taking care of me that I wanted it to go on and on. For one minute I laid aside all the things that were weighing so heavy on me. Sister Therese reached over and smoothed my cheek with her hand. Then she pushed my bangs off my forehead. "Don't worry," she whispered, smiling all the while. "Everything will be fine."

"You're awful nice," I said. She pulled the blankets up to my chin and winked.

"Just doing my job," she said. I remembered what Wendy'd said about nuns having to be nice to everyone and smiled. It was true. "They're bringing your breakfast now," said Sister Therese. "I'd better go."

"Thanks," I said, wishing she didn't have to go. Selfish me, I thought an instant later. Nurses have a lot of people to take care of, not just Bobbie Lynn Brewer. The nun's gown rustled softly as she turned to go out the door. "I know a baby named Therese," I added.

"I know," she said. She waved from the door and I waved back, and not one minute later another nurse brought in a tray of food. She was a sister too. Sister Agnes Kemp it said on her name tag, but she wore a different outfit. Hers was blue and didn't go all the way to the floor like Sister Therese's did. How could there be so many kinds of nuns? This Catholic business was confusing. I'd have a pile of questions to ask Wendy next time I saw her.

At first I didn't want anything to eat, but then when Sister Agnes lifted the lid from the bacon and eggs and uncovered a bowl of hot oatmeal, all of a sudden I realized I was hungry enough to eat a horse, hooves and all. The doctor came in just as I'd finished. Another nurse was with him. She was dressed like Sister Agnes. She moved the tray away but didn't leave the room. She pulled a big green curtain all the way around my bed.

"I'm Doctor Anthony Kearney," said the man in the white coat, "but most of my patients call me Doctor Tony." He smiled. "I have a little girl just your age," he said. He looked in my ears and down my throat. He talked the whole time he examined me. "She goes to St. Leo's. Where do you go?"

"Fawcett Elementary," I said. He sat me up and put his stethoscope on my back. It was cold. Suddenly I wondered who'd changed my clothes. I didn't remember getting undressed.

"My oldest daughter, that's the one your age, is named Brigit. How many in your family?"

"Two of us," I said. The stethoscope was cold on my chest. "My brother and me is all."

"Breathe," said the doctor. "Now I know it hurts, but cough a little for me." I did as he asked. He moved the stethoscope around and had me breathe two more times. I was glad when he took it away and the nurse tied my gown back up around my neck.

"Well, Bobbie Lynn," said Dr. Tony, "you've got pneumonia. But here's the good news. It's not viral, like I thought at first. We started you on penicillin last night—that's what's in the IV—and your fever is already gone. Outstanding. Really, quite amazing. Are you coughing up a lot of phlegm?" I nodded. "Great," said Dr. Tony.

I coughed three or four times. My cough hurt less this morning than it had the night before. And I *was* coughing up big gobs of stuff.

"Good-sounding cough, really," said Dr. Tony. He was grinning again and rocking back and forth on his feet. I noticed he had a lot of freckles, like a kid. I wondered if Brigit had freckles too. "Now all you need are rest and more antibiotics, and if you're really a good girl and get well as fast as I think you can, I'll send you home tomorrow or the next day."

"What about my mother?" I asked. "Can I see her?" Dr. Tony frowned.

"Oh, that's right, we can't send you home until your mom is better." He scratched his head and frowned. "But I think I remember someone saying something about relatives. I think so. Or was it friends? Hmm. I'll have to check. I'm sure everything will work out. We won't send you home to nobody." Dr. Tony chuckled. "No, we'll take good care of you. Oh, and about seeing your mother, let me check with her doctor. Is that A-OK?" He patted my hand.

Before I could ask any more questions there was a knock. The nurse left my bedside and stepped outside the curtain. In a few seconds she put her head back inside and said, "Bobbie Lynn has visitors, Doctor."

"Fine, fine," said Dr. Tony. He pulled back the curtain and there was Mason. "You must be the brother," said Dr. Tony. "I'll let you two chat." He left and the nurse left with him.

"Hi, stupid," said Mason.

"Hey, you ugly pig," I said. Tears flooded my eyes. I never thought I'd be so glad to see that boy, glad enough to hug and kiss him if I'd dared. "What are you doing here? How did you get out of juvenile hall?"

"I never went."

"Isn't that why the policeman was there? I saw him. He came to take you away to juvenile hall."

"They didn't take me. I told them I wouldn't go where there's no color TV."

. "Stop that! Where did you sleep last night? I was so worried. Have you seen Mama?" I tried to sit up but it made me cough. "What are we going to do, Mason? They said I can go home tomorrow or the next day, but if no one is home, they'll take us to the juvenile hall, or a foster home!" All the thoughts that I'd worried over flooded my brain. If I could have, I would have grabbed Mason and shook him. I hated him just then. How could he make jokes? "Don't tease me," I said.

Mason sat on the edge of the bed and leaned toward me. "Just shut your yap and listen up for one minute, will you?" I clamped my mouth shut and swiped at my eyes with my free hand. "Remember when the phone was ringing last night?"

"Yeah. And we didn't pick it up."

"Well it rang again, after they took you and Mama out to the ambulance." Mason moved his face so close to mine that I could smell toothpaste on his breath. He took my chin in his hand. He held me there and looked me in the eye. "Listen up, Bobbie, will you?"

"What?"

"It was about Daddy."

Chapter Nineteen

"You lie," I said and turned my face away so Mason couldn't see how scared I was.

Tell me the truth. No, don't.

"No, no, I'm not lying. I'm sick of lying, aren't you?"

"Sick to pieces," I said. I looked into my brother's blue-green eyes, the eyes that were crying as bad as mine were now. Lying eyes don't look like that. I swallowed and sniffed and tried not to breathe out of control, tried not to cough. "What about him?" I whispered.

"They found him. Alive."

How could it be true? It was too good to be true. My brother did something he'd never done. He opened his skinny arms and pulled me to himself in a big hug. "It's true," he whispered. "He's alive." When Mason said "alive" his voice squeaked.

"Is he okay?" I asked through my tears.

"He's sick—he has malaria real bad. That's why he couldn't call us himself. And he broke his ankle. He had to have surgery, but he's going to be okay. His commander called us on a ham-radio patch."

"Where is he?"

"He's in Bangkok," said Mason. "In Thailand. Bobbie Lynn, the commander said Daddy saved two other guys. He broke his ankle carrying one of them away from gunfire."

I was stunned, like someone had hit me over the head with a brick. My ears started to buzz, like they had just before I fainted the night before. Daddy was alive! I panicked from the fainting feeling and pushed Mason away so I could lie back on the bed. I coughed several times and realized I'd been holding my breath. Stupid me.

"The commander said he tried to call several times earlier. He said he let it ring a bunch of times but no one answered."

I felt a surge of guilt over leaving Mama for the whole afternoon. If anyone had tried to call, she wouldn't have been able to answer.

"Does Mama know?" I asked.

"I don't know. They wouldn't let me see her," said Mason. He looked away and fiddled with a string on his sleeve button. "She can't have visitors, not even Mrs. Feeney. She's on the floor above here." He pointed up at the ceiling. "I talked to her doctor some."

What was he keeping from me?

"Tell me what he said," I urged. Mason grabbed a Kleenex out of the box by my bed.

"I never had so much snot in all my life," he said. He blew his nose with a honk and grinned. Then he pulled another Kleenex out and handed it to me. "You look horrible."

"Shut up," I said, but I didn't mean it in a sassy way.

"Isn't it great about Daddy?" For a second I forgot my

worry about Mama. How could so many feelings come at once? They washed over me again like an ocean wave. Daddy was safe! We had to tell Mama right away! She'd be thrilled to bits.

"Where did you stay last night?" I asked for the second time. "And how did you get downtown to see me?"

"I'll tell you, just hold your horses," said Mason. He seemed relieved that I wasn't asking about Mama. I felt a dark cloud of worry beginning to build in my heart but I pushed it away. Mason darted across the room and out the door. He came back in with Mrs. Feeney. "I stayed with your friends. And Mrs. Feeney brought me here."

"Hi, Bobbie Lynn," said Wendy's mom. She smiled and came over to pat my hand. "You look so much better, dear."

"Thank you, ma'am," I said. "Thank you for helping last night."

"When I got your call in the middle of the night, I called the police department and hurried right over. You scared me to death! But what wonderful news about your father."

"Yes, it is," I said. "And thanks for taking in my fleabag brother." Mason stuck his tongue out at me.

"My husband and I told the policeman that we were friends of the family," said Mrs. Feeney, "and he seemed relieved not to have to take Mason."

"'Cuz my reputation precedes me," said Mason, taking a bow.

"They sent a social worker by today," said Mrs. Feeney. "It's all arranged. You can come to our house until your aunt gets here."

I stared at Mason.

"Aunt Jeri Lee, who else?" he said.

"You called her?" I couldn't believe my ears.

"Yeah, I did," said Mason. "She said she and Matthew Mark'd be here by the end of the week. They're taking the Greyhound. Her boss at the beauty parlor gave her a month off on account of Daddy being her brother and a war hero and all. She said Matthew Mark can do his schoolwork up here as well as in Austin. Aunt Jeri Lee said it's about time her and Mama make up, and besides, she wants to be around when Daddy gets in."

"Daddy's coming back?" I asked, feeling bewildered and happy at the same time. My head was swirling at high speed from all the thoughts and feelings coming at once. An aunt we'd never met was coming to take care of us. What would she be like? Daddy wasn't missing anymore, he was fine, he was safe, he was alive! But I hadn't thought he would come home. He was supposed to be gone a whole year.

"They're giving him a ninety-day leave," said Mason. "Maybe more depending on how his ankle heals up. Didn't I tell you that?"

Ninety days. Three months. Mama had to know. She'd get better for sure if she knew that.

Just then Sister Agnes Kemp came back into the room. She put her hand on my head and felt my pulse. She looked at my face and frowned a little.

"I think we need a rest," she said.

"She's excited from some good news about our father," said Mason.

"I heard," said the nurse, with a smile.

"Sister is right," said Mrs. Feeney. She squeezed my hand. "You take a nap and do everything they tell you. I'll come back tomorrow when they release you."

"Can Wendy visit me today?" I asked. "And Jean?"

"No," said Mrs. Feeney. "Children aren't supposed to visit. They made an exception for Mason." Sister Agnes and Mrs. Feeney exchanged looks. "Let's go, Mason," said Mrs. Feeney. "Thank you, Sister," she said. "And thank that nice doctor too." So Dr. Tony had let them bring Mason in to see me. He'd known all along that children visiting was against the rules and he never said a word.

"See you tomorrow," said Mason, looking at the nurse, "if I can sneak in again."

"I get to leave tomorrow," I said. And then added, "Maybe. If I'm good."

"My little sister's never good, ma'am," said Mason to the nurse. "Guess y'all will have to keep her forever."

"You rest now," said Mrs. Feeney. "Oh! I nearly forgot." She opened her purse and pulled out a pink envelope. "Wendy was quite angry about not being able to visit."

"I imagine so," I said.

"She asked me to give you this." Mrs. Feeney handed me the envelope.

"Thank you," I said, "and tell Wendy thank you too."

"I will," said Mrs. Feeney. "You get well."

"Yeah," said Mason, trying to sound bossy. "We mean it."

"Shut up," I said, but I smiled when I said it.

"I'd say she's back to normal," said Mason, and everyone laughed, including me.

* * *

Sister Agnes gave me a sponge bath and put new sheets on my bed. It felt like heaven to have someone else take care of me. I hoped Mama had nurses this nice. Sister Agnes chatted about this and that but I thought about Daddy and Mama the whole time. Twice I had tears in my eyes and Sister Agnes thought it was because I was in pain. Both times she asked, "Does it hurt?" and I shook my head. I didn't have the energy to tell her they were happy tears. Actually, they were only partly happy tears. How could I be completely happy about Daddy with Mama so sick? Why hadn't Mason told me everything about Mama? And what would Daddy say when he saw the holes in the ceiling? I forgot all about Wendy's note until the nurse left the room. I took it from the bedside stand. Her tight little handwriting covered both sides of the paper.

Dear Bobbie Lynn:

Right now I just finished breakfast and Mom says I have to go to school instead of come to see you in the hospital. I was so mad I stomped my foot, which got me a week of no cold cereal, only toast and oatmeal in the morning and a bad-temper lecture. It is not my fault Therese was right under me when I stomped. You should have heard her scream. I didn't mean to hurt her. I told my mom it's a good thing I have a bad temper or I'd never have anything to tell Father Andrevich at confession on Saturdays and then she said Do You Want To Be Grounded For A Month Young Lady? and I said no but I was still mad. Stevie was glad about no cold cereal because that means more Cocoa Puffs for him. He actually started to count

them in his bowl, just to prove he had more because I did-
n't get any. He is THE WEIRDEST BROTHER IN
THE WORLD and I am so mad at him. Anyway, I can't
visit you because children have more germs. So here is a
letter instead. Mom told me everything that happened to
you, E-V-E-R-Y-T-H-I-N-G including your dad being
being found (yeah!) and your mom being sick (boo!) and
etc etc etc. #1. I'm going to yell at you FOR NOT
TELLING how your mom was having certain problems.
OK, maybe you thought you'd better not. This is what
friends are for, but maybe you didn't know that. Now I'm
done yelling at you. (Right here, imagine me smiling
instead.) #2. You get to stay at our house YABBA
DABBA DOO. You can have my bed and I can sleep on
the floor. It will be like camping. #3. Jean asked to go
back to the convent to see the doves. No one believes me,
but it's true. She said "bub" first thing this morning and
that's how I knew. #4. We aren't moving back to
Pittsburgh after all. I guess I'll just have to put up with
Debbie And Company but that's life. Maybe I will stop
getting so mad at them and become a Nice Young Lady
instead. Yuck. I like fighting better (just kidding). #5. I
said two whole rosaries plus the guardian-angel prayer
ten times for your dad. And HA HA the guardian
angels WERE DOING THEIR JOB. Now you have to
believe me.

Your friend 4-ever,
Wendy Kathleen Feeney, esq.

I read the letter three times. Then I folded it and put it
back in its envelope. Wendy was right. The guardian

angels had done their job, at least so far. I put the letter under my pillow and tried to rest. Daddy was safe, our house had not burned down from cigarettes, Mason wasn't at juvenile hall, and I wouldn't have to go there either because Aunt Jeri Lee was coming.

But what about Mama?

Chapter Twenty

Around dinnertime Dr. Tony came back. "I found out about your mom," he said as he thumped my back in three places and listened. "Dr. Bradford is her doctor. He said there is good reason to hope for a full recovery. He's already started her on some medications that should help a lot."

Hope? Dr. Tony asked me to cough. What did he mean by hope? "Your lungs sound good," he said. "You'll cough for a while, and you'll have to rest. Any questions?" asked Dr. Tony.

"May I see my mother?" I asked. Dr. Tony shook his head.

"She's in the psychiatric ward," he said. "Do you know what that means?" I nodded. Everyone knew what that meant.

"She isn't ready for visitors, Bobbie Lynn. Not yet. But she will be, I promise."

"Can they help a person whose mind is—delicate, um, and—can they get her back to normal?" A big sob jumped up into my throat and choked off my words. Would Mama ever go back to normal? The way she was when we were little and she didn't have her spells? That's what I wanted to know.

Dr. Tony scratched the side of his face with one finger. "Your brother talked to Dr. Bradford for some time this morning. He told the doctor everything." Dr. Tony looked right at me and smiled, but it was a sad smile. Part of me felt relieved. Part of me felt like a traitor. We'd worked so hard to keep Mama's problems private.

There wasn't any secret anymore.

Everything in the room got blurry-looking. Dr. Tony sat beside me. He spoke quietly and his breath smelled like coffee. "Your mother has been suffering from a great deal of anxiety, you know, being way more worried than is normal."

"She gets worried a lot," I said. Dr. Tony nodded.

"That's what your brother said. And Dr. Bradford thinks she is depressed as well, you know, sad a lot of the time, all out of energy, that sort of thing."

"And medicine can help?" I asked.

"Yes," said Dr. Tony, "and maybe some other therapy as well. That will be up to Dr. Bradford."

"So you think Mama will get better, really and truly?"

"Little by little," said Dr. Tony. "Dr. Bradford takes care of patients like your mother all the time. It's his specialty, and if he didn't think there was hope he would-n't say so."

"Does she know about Daddy being found?" I asked. "She has to know."

"Dr. Bradford will tell her as soon as she is awake enough to understand," said Dr. Tony. "As soon as it's the right time to tell her about your dad, I know he'll give her that great news. And let you and your brother see her too."

"All right then," I said. "I'll be patient."

"That's a girl," said Dr. Tony. He messed up my hair and tweaked my nose. "Brigit's got that same haircut," he said. "It's called a pixie, isn't it?"

"That's right, sir," I said.

"Cute as can be," said Dr. Tony, and then he hurried out the door.

I had to stay an extra day because my cough was still bad. I didn't mind. Even though I couldn't see Mama yet it was nice to know she was close. The nurses were all nice as pie. Lots of them were nuns, and some were just regular nurses. I kept hoping Sister Therese would come back to see me, but she never did. I didn't see any other nurses all dressed in white either.

The next day Dr. Tony said I could come home, and Mrs. Feeney came right at two o'clock. She even brought some of my own clothes from our house so I wouldn't have to go home in my pajamas. I would have been happier to leave the hospital if I'd been able to see Mama, but the nurse who pushed my wheelchair out to the taxi said I could call the nurses' station any time and find out how she was doing. That made me feel a little better.

When we got to Wendy's house Wendy and Stevie were still at school. Mrs. Feeney said Mason was at school too. I wondered if she'd written his excuse note. Mr. Feeney was sitting on Jean's sofa and Jean was sitting on his lap. They were playing pat-a-cake. I should say

Mr. Feeney was playing. Jean just swung her arms, but maybe for her that was playing. Therese was crawling across the front-room floor with a stuffed teddy bear hanging from her mouth.

"Spit out the bear, Therese," Mrs. Feeney scolded, and then she helped me go upstairs to Wendy's room. "You heard the doctor say bed rest for a week. Wendy begged to sleep on the floor beside you, but if she talks too much, let me know and I'll move her."

"Yes, ma'am," I said. "I don't think I'll mind her." Mrs. Feeney gave me one of her own nightgowns.

"Wendy's would be too small," she said. "I'll have Mason run home and get some more things tonight. I completely forgot to pick up a nightgown for you." Mrs. Feeney left the room so I could undress. I slipped my clothes off and put on the flannel gown. Mrs. Feeney was about my height but she was a lot rounder. The nightgown was baggy but at least it didn't drag. I crawled between the covers of Wendy's bed and closed my eyes. How could I be so tired after being in bed so much? It felt good and soon I dozed off, but I awakened with a start when I sensed that someone was standing right next to me. It was Wendy.

"I didn't make a sound," she said. "How did you know I was here?"

"I don't know," I said. "I just knew. You startled me."

"Sorry." Wendy folded her hands behind her back and stared at me. Her face was flushed and her hair was every which way.

"Did you run home?" I asked.

"Yep," she said. "How are you feeling?"

"I don't have a fever and I feel fine except for this cough and being dead tired. And the doctor says I'm not contagious, on account of the penicillin."

"Oh, good," said Wendy. "Did you get my letter?"

"Yes," I said. "I read it a bunch of times."

"Mom said it was too long. She said it would make you tired to read it."

"No, it was just right," I said.

"Stevie really likes your brother," said Wendy. "The two of them are building a Tinkertoy thing. Your brother says it's an air force jet but Stevie says it looks more like a spaceship. Stevie got mad because when he said that astronauts are going to land on the Moon real soon, Mason said that's horse manure." The thought of Mason arguing with Stevie made me giggle. Giggling made me cough, but it didn't hurt this time.

"I'm glad your dad is coming back," said Wendy.

"Me too."

"Hey, wait up!" I heard Stevie yell. I heard some thumping on the stairs and the next thing I knew Mason was at the door of Wendy's bedroom. Stevie came up behind him panting.

"Hi, stupid," said Mason.

"Hey, ugly," I said.

"I heard they gave you penicillin shots," said Stevie, pushing past Mason into the room. "Did they give you a million cc's?"

"Shut up," said Wendy. "Can't you see Bobbie Lynn is an invalid right now?"

"It's all right," I said. "I don't know how much penicillin they gave me, Stevie. All I know is it feels like a mule kicked me in the behind." Everyone laughed at that.

"Stephen, Wendy, come away," called Mrs. Feeney from downstairs. Stevie squeezed out past Mason.

"See ya," said Wendy, and disappeared out the door.

"You fine?" Mason asked me.

"Uh-huh," I said. "Talk to Mama yet?"

"No." He shook his head and looked down. "But guess what! A kid in my class said he'd teach me his paper route today. He's going to quit and I can have the job if I want it. I said I'd take it. I'd better get or I'll be late."

"Maybe you can get your bike back," I said. Mason grinned.

"Yeah, maybe, but I have some other things to pay back first, y'know?" His cheeks turned pink.

"Good idea," I said. I wanted to say more. I wanted to say I was proud of him for doing the right thing but I couldn't get the words out just then. Maybe later.

"Aunt Jeri Lee'll be here in two days. She called from Kansas City."

"What's she like?" I asked. I felt nervous about meeting Aunt Jeri Lee. Mama'd said so many bad things about her. But she was kin, and maybe it was time her and Mama let bygones be bygones.

"She seems nice enough," said Mason. "She talks fast and if something tickles her, she kinda hoots. Like this." Mason fake-giggled and laughed and then at the end he hooted real funny. It made me laugh. "I like her, on the phone, that is," he said.

Maybe if Mason liked her on the phone, I'd like her too. Maybe even Mama could like her, in time. "You

think that medicine they're giving Mama will help?"
I asked.

"I'm counting on it," said Mason. "That and the news
about Daddy. I wish they'd let us tell her."

"Me too," I said. "Or else I wish they'd tell her themselves." Mason nodded but he didn't say anything. I
think we both knew there wasn't a single thing either of
us could do to make Mama get well. We'd tried and we'd
failed, and now it was out of our hands. I hoped like anything that those doctors knew what they were doing.

"Well, I have to go do that paper route. See you at
suppertime," said Mason.

"Okay," I said, and Mason was gone. Before I had two
seconds to think over what we'd talked about, Wendy
came in and sat on the edge of the bed.

"Isn't it boring in bed?"

"Yeah, pretty much," I said.

"How about if I bring Jean up? I haven't really talked
to her today. She lies around all day too." Before I could
say yes or no, Wendy had leaped up from the bed and I
heard her running down the stairs. In a few minutes she
reappeared. Her dad was behind her with Jean in his
arms. There was an old, tattered, green recliner chair in
the corner of Wendy's room. Wendy flipped out the
footrest and pushed the back into the recline position.
Mr. Feeney plopped Jean down into the chair and left,
smiling at me on the way out.

"Who's that, Jean?" said Wendy. "Who is that in
my bed?" Jean had begun to drool so Wendy pulled
out one of her dresser drawers and pulled out a clean

white undershirt. She wiped Jean's mouth. "Who's that?" she asked.

"Hey, Jean," I said. "It's me, Bobbie Lynn." Jean swung her head in the direction of my voice.

"Wah."

"Hi, yourself," I said, and Wendy and I both laughed.

"Who's this, Jean?" asked Wendy. She was sitting on the arm of the chair. She leaned way over and picked up one of Jean's hands. She put it on her own head. "Who's this? Who's me?" Wendy kissed Jean's little hand and put it back at her side. "She never makes a sound when I ask her that," said Wendy. "But I know she knows it's me."

"Tee," said Jean.

Wendy and I stared at Jean and then looked at each other.

"She never said that before," said Wendy.

"What do you think it means?" Wendy shrugged and knelt next to the chair.

"Who's this, Jean?" Wendy put Jean's hand on her cheek. Jean's blind blue eyes roamed from side to side. "Who's me?"

"Tee," said Jean again.

"Wen-dee?" squeaked Wendy. Jean listened. "Katie?" Jean jerked her hand away and squealed.

"Tee-tee-tee-tee-tee-tee-tee." Jean started to laugh. It was that same laugh I'd heard the first time Wendy and I whistled for the doves, the one that had been so funny I'd had to stop whistling. Wendy laughed and clapped her hands.

"She said it! I know it was me she meant. I *know* it!"

Wendy did a little dance in a circle. "Tee! That's me!" All of a sudden she stopped and sat beside me on the bed. I saw something I'd never seen in her eyes. I saw tears. "It's a miracle, Bobbie Lynn. Just like when she said 'birds.'"

"I believe you're right," I said.

"Tee-tee-tee-tee-tee," said Jean. Wendy jumped up.

"Mom!" she yelled, and ran out the door.

Soon the whole Feeney family was crowded into Wendy's room. "Watch," said Wendy. She put Jean's hand on her face. "Who's this?" she asked. "Katie?"

"Tee," said Jean. Mrs. Feeney gasped.

"Oh my goodness," she whispered.

"Daddy, come here," said Wendy. Mr. Feeney squatted down beside the chair. Wendy put Jean's hand on her father's face. "Who's this, Jean?"

"Da."

"And who's me?"

"Tee-tee-tee."

"Sweet Mother of God!" whispered Mr. Feeney. "Jeannie girl's talking!" The look on his face was so happy and surprised at the same time that we all laughed. Did I see tears in his eyes too?

All the Feeneys started to talk at once, until Mrs. Feeney looked over at me. "Oh, poor Bobbie Lynn! She's supposed to be resting. Katie, I told you not to bother her."

"It's all right, ma'am," I said. "I was bored stiff." The Feeneys laughed again. Jean even joined in laughing. When she started to squeal really loud, Mrs. Feeney tried to shush her but it didn't work.

"Now you have to go back to your old identity, *Katie*," said Stevie.

"All right, already," said Wendy. "But only because of Jean." She put her hand on Jean's cheek.

"Tee!" hollered Jean.

"That's it. Everyone downstairs," said Mrs. Feeney. Mr. Feeney lifted Jean out of the recliner. Therese leaned over from Mrs. Feeney's arms and grabbed a handful of Stevie's hair.

"OW!" he cried.

"I bet you wish you'd stayed at the hospital, huh, Bobbie Lynn?" said Wendy. "Our house is pretty noisy all the time."

"No, this is just fine," I said. I snuggled down into the covers while everyone left the room. "It's happy noise."

"I guess you'll have to call me Katie too, so Jean won't be confused."

"Whatever you like," I said. "It's your name. But it might take me a while to switch. I think of you as Wendy."

"Okay, how about if you start next week, since you aren't used to it."

"That'd be good," I said.

"Katie is who I am. You know. My real identity."

"Not just your Pittsburgh identity?"

"No, my Tacoma-Stinky-Aroma identity too."

"You make a good Katie," I said.

"Now you can get to know the Katie me," she said, "which is mostly like the Wendy me." We both laughed.

"I'm sure I'll like the Katie you," I said, not wanting to explain how I'd hidden so much from her from the very start, how I'd wanted to tell her everything but couldn't, why all her talk about angels gave me the willies because I didn't dare think long about Daddy being in danger. There would be plenty of time for us to get to know our real-identity selves. Right then, I was starting to feel bushed.

"Thank you so much, Bobbie Lynn," said Wendy. She put her arms around me and gave me a big hug.

"For what?" I asked.

"For being here. So Jean would want to show off. She loves to show off for you." She closed the door quietly behind herself.

I thought about her for a long time after she left, Wendy Katie Feeney, the wild girl who whistled for doves and threw dirt at kids who teased. The girl who liked to skip because it was almost like flying. Maybe I'd try skipping when I was feeling better. Why not? We could have a skipping contest, see who could skip the highest. Wendy'd like that.

Wendy had such a terrible temper and just about the biggest heart I'd ever known. Could anyone love a sister as much as she loved Jean? It would take a while to think of Wendy as Katie but I'd try hard and pretty soon it would come.

Sister Mary Clara had said something about knowing Jean's guardian angel and suddenly I realized exactly what she'd meant. She'd been talking about Wendy! Wendy's was the face she'd seen. Wendy's was the face of Jean's angel. I thought about that. Angels don't just fly around in heaven, then, like Mama'd said. Sometimes they come alongside when a person needs it most.

An angel can come as an old, old nun who lets you feed grain to her beautiful birds or promises to say a prayer for your dad and then says "please come back and visit me." An angel can come along looking like an ugly older brother who buys you a licorice whip, or one can come when you make a phone call in the middle of the night and ask for help. An angel might sit beside your hospital bed when your own mom is too sick to be there or call you "dear" and feel your forehead and smile at you until your aches and pains seem small.

Sometimes an angel writes you a long letter on pink paper or gives you a sponge bath without making you feel embarrassed to be naked, or tells you your ugly hair-cut is cute. Sometimes an angel gives your brother a paper-route job, or loans you a nightgown, or makes you laugh by showing off when you just got out of the hospital.

Sometimes an angel calls from Thailand to tell you your daddy is going to be fine.

Daddy'd been an angel too, for that hurt man who'd needed carrying. So had I, and so had Mason. We'd been angels for Mama when she needed us most.

Baby Angel. It's what Daddy always called me. He'd be glad I'd asked for help. I knew he would.

Wendy was telling the truth all along. I could believe it now. There really were angels all around. And maybe God was nearby too.

Far away downstairs I heard the telephone ring. Someone picked it up after four rings. "MOM!" Stevie yelled. "DAD?" I closed my eyes and let myself sink into the pillow. What a noisy house!

I hadn't rested ten seconds before someone was

knocking furiously on the door. "Come in," I said. Wendy burst in out of breath, her eyes wide with excitement.

"It's for you" she said. "It's your *mom!* She wants to talk to you!"

"Mama?" I whispered. I hardly had time to sit up before Mr. Feeney stuck his head around the door.

"Need help down the stairs?" he asked.

"Yes, please," I said. "Thank you." Wendy helped me out of bed and handed me a bathrobe.

"Here," she said. "Wear my new bathrobe. I got it for my birthday. It'll keep you warm and cozy." Wendy's bathrobe was pink and fuzzy and I could tell by looking that it was way too short for me. I put it on anyhow.

Mr. Feeney put his arm around me and helped me down the stairs. Wendy's little bathrobe kept me warm and cozy the whole time, just like she'd said it would.

Angel of God,
my guardian, dear,
to whom God's love
commits me here;
ever this day
be at my side,
to light, to guard,
to rule, to guide.

Amen

ALSO BY KRISTINE L. FRANKLIN

Lone Wolf

Paperback ISBN 0-7636-2996-0

Grape Thief

Hardcover ISBN 0-7636-1325-8

Available wherever books are sold